JULES VERNE (1828–1905) was born in Nantes, France. He wrote over sixty novels, and is famous for his fascination with science and travel. He is the author of such well-known classics as *Journey to the Centre of the Earth*, *Around the World in Eighty Days* and *Twenty Thousand Leagues under the Sea*. In 1859 Verne travelled to Scotland, a journey that inspired this novel and influenced many of his other works.

D0767281

The cover photograph, *Loch Katrine, Autumn 1844*, is by William Henry Fox Talbot. One of the first photographs taken of Scotland, it comes from Talbot's *Sun Pictures in Scotland*, one of the first photography books, of which only 19 copies remain. Reproduced courtesy of the University of Michigan Museum of Art. Museum purchase made possible by the Friends of the Museum of Art 1980/1.144.

Inside illustrations are the original engravings by Charles Barbant of J Férat's drawings from the first edition of *Les Indes noires* by Jules Verne, Paris 1877. Reproduced courtesy of the Trustees of the National Library of Scotland.

LES
INDES NOIRES
Jules VERNE
45 DESSINS PAR J. FÉRAT

The Underground City

A new translation of the complete text with illustrations

JULES VERNE

translated by Sarah Crozier
with a foreword by Professor Ian Thompson

Luath Press Limited
EDINBURGH
www.luath.co.uk

First published as *Les Indes noires*, Paris 1877
First published in English as *Child of the Cavern* or
Strange Doings Underground, London 1877
This translation first published 2005

The paper used in this book is recyclable. It is made from
low-chlorine pulps produced in a low-energy, low-emission
manner from renewable forests.

Printed and bound by
Nørhaven, Viborg, Denmark

Typeset in Sabon 10.5 by Sarah Crozier, Nantes

Contents

LES VOYAGES EXTRAORDINAIRES

LES INDES-NOIRES

PAR

JULES VERNE

DESSINS PAR J. FÉRAT, GRAVURES PAR CHARLES BARBANT

BIBLIOTHÈQUE
D'ÉDUCATION ET DE RÉCRÉATION
J. HETZEL ET Cⁱᵉ, 18, RUE JACOB
PARIS

Title page from the original 1877 edition of Les Indes noires

Translator's Note

DESPITE HIS TRAVELS in Scotland, and knowing the difference between the various parts of the United Kingdom, Verne, like many of his compatriots, is occasionally guilty of using 'England' and 'the English' to refer to Britain and the British, or even Scotland and the Scottish. Where an ambiguity or a contradiction arises these terms have been changed accordingly. The wrongly identified 'Grampians' have been changed to 'the Trossachs'. Place name spellings and words quoted by Verne in English have also been corrected.

Les Indes noires (literally '*The Black Indies*') was extensively rewritten following the demands of Verne's editor Jules Hetzel. The plot was considerably reworked, changing amongst other things the time in which the novel is set and the importance of certain characters, and some chapters were completely excised. No doubt in part because of this, there are various inconsistencies in the text, such as inconsistencies in time. Where these are particularly confusing, the text has been amended.

Following other recent English translations of Verne's work, some of the many exclamation marks have been removed. Where Verne has quoted from Sir Walter Scott, the latter's original text has been used.

The text used is the Hetzel edition. It is full and unabridged, and the footnotes are Verne's.

Acknowledgements are due to the Centre d'études Vernienne in Nantes, George Archibald from the Scottish Mining Museum, William Butcher, Robert Crozier, Katya Melluish and Professor Ian Thompson for their comments and suggestions.

SC

Foreword

TOWARDS MIDNIGHT on Friday 26 August 1859, the Caledonian Railway express from Liverpool pulled into Edinburgh's Lothian Road terminus. As the smoke and steam cleared, two men emerged. One of them was Jules Verne, then aged 31 and practically unknown but who was to become the fourth most translated author in the world. With him was a musician friend, Aristide Hignard, who was to be Verne's companion on their brief tour of Scotland. As he stepped onto the platform so Verne took a crucial step in his lifelong love affair with Scotland and the Scots. Few Scots today are aware of the famous author's special connection with their country. In fact, Verne claimed Scottish ancestry on his mother's side, from a fifteenth century archer, N. Allott, in the service of Louis XI of France. Having served the king with distinction, he was awarded the noble title of 'de la Fuÿe', signifying the right to own a dovecot, and the family name became 'Allotte de la Fuÿe'. Moreover, from his youth, Verne had revelled in the works of Sir Walter Scott, popularised in Europe by the Romantic movement, which Verne had read avidly in translation. He had delved widely into Scottish history and as a Breton, sympathised with the notion of Scotland, like Ireland, as being downtrodden and exploited by the English.

This absorption with all things Scottish is reflected in his fiction. Two novels are entirely set in Scotland, *Les Indes noires* and *Le Rayon vert*, and three others are located in part in Scotland. Moreover, Verne delighted in populating his novels with Scottish characters, invariably cast in a heroic mould as aristocrats, mariners, explorers or tycoons. At least 40 Scots feature in his adventure novels as major or minor characters. However, it is doubtful if Scotland would have featured so prominently in his work had Verne not had an opportunity to visit the country unexpectedly in 1859. At this time, having qualified as a lawyer in Paris and recently married, Verne was in fact more interested in writing for the theatre. In 1859, the brother of his friend Hignard offered the pair a sea passage to Liverpool and thus an opportunity to visit Scotland. Verne set off in great excitement. This was to be his first journey abroad and his first encounter with mountains and lakes. The visit to Scotland lasted only five days but he did not waste a moment; we must consider it in some detail since it coloured his future writing on Scotland and the plot of *Les Indes noires* in particular. Indeed some critics consider that his encounter with Scotland was to provide a template for the series of over 60 novels known as the *Voyages Extraordinaires*. These novels blend travel, adventure, exoticism, historical detail and scientific imagination in specific geographical regions. While in most cases, the creations were the produce of painstaking research, his Scottish novels were born of firsthand experience. In this sense we may claim that Verne is at his most authentic when writing about Scotland.

On the day after their arrival, the friends spent the morning exploring the Old Town and as they followed the Royal Mile, Verne regaled Hignard with scenes from Scott's *Heart of Midlothian*. After recounting historical events at Holyrood Palace, Verne ascended Arthur's Seat, his first 'mountain'. The view from the summit filled Verne with amazement and in his account of their journey[i] he concludes an emotional description with the sentence 'No pen can do justice to this breathtaking scene'. The two friends descend to Portobello and a numbing swim before returning to the city centre. They make their way through the New Town to Inverleith Row where a distant relative of Hignard, a prominent businessman, resided close to the Botanic Gardens. Verne was charmed by the eldest daughter, Amelia, and she agreed to draft an itinerary for a visit to the

---

[i] Verne's account of his travels in England and Scotland was published posthumously in France in 1989 and in translation in English in 1992 as *Backwards to Britain*, Chambers, Edinburgh.

Highlands, which Verne ardently wished to see. A dinner guest was a Catholic priest, the Reverend Smith, who insisted that they should visit him at his brother's castle in Fife on their journey. The following day, the two friends continued exploring the Old Town before returning to Inverleith Row where Amelia handed over her itinerary and the Reverend Smith repeated his invitation to lunch.

Thus, the following morning, Verne and his companion boarded the Stirling steamer at Granton Pier in the teeth of a gale and pouring rain. They disembarked with difficulty at Crombie Point in Fife where, as promised, the priest met them and they walked to Inzievar House near Oakley, the 'castle' belonging to his brother. Verne marvelled at the modernity of the newly built mansion and from its rooftop observed the estate, coal mine and ironworks that were at the origin of the Smith family's wealth. After a hearty lunch and having dried their clothes, Verne and Hignard caught the train to Glasgow via Stirling and lodged at a hotel on George Square. On the following morning, 30 August, the friends explored the cathedral and necropolis, the city centre and the harbour. As compared with Edinburgh, which Verne found magnificent, Glasgow impressed him less though he admired the energy of its industry and port trade and the bustle of the city centre. However, Verne was impatient to head for the Highlands. After lunch, the train was caught to Balloch at the southern tip of Loch Lomond and the pair boarded the *SS Prince Albert*. At once Verne waxed lyrical on the scenery and the stories of the struggles between the MacGregors and Colquhouns and agreed with Scott's opinion that 'Loch Lomond is the fairest of lochs and Ben Lomond the monarch of mountains'. At last, the steamer reached Inversnaid near the head of the loch and after a whisky at the inn, they mounted a coach which took them to Stronachlachar pier on Loch Katrine where the *Rob Roy* was waiting to sail its passengers to the Trossachs. Apart from marvelling at the majestic scenery, Verne now turned his commentary to the supernatural, the goblins and fairies which reportedly populated the shores of the loch. Finally, on disembarking, Verne turned round 'one last time to bid goodbye to those magnificent landscapes whose sublime beauty defies the imagination'.

The remainder of their journey was unremarkable. They spent the night in Stirling and proceeded to Edinburgh the following day where, after revisiting for a last time their favourite streets in the Old Town, they caught the overnight train to London. This précis of Verne's first visit to Scotland is essential in order to understand the action in *Les Indes noires* and as can be seen from the map, the itineraries taken in the plot correspond in detail to Verne's own travel in 1859.

The focus of the novel is an 'underground city', a vast coal mine abandoned as being exhausted then revived on the discovery of vast new seams. A new coalfield, 'New Aberfoyle' is opened and rapidly 'Coal City' is built in a huge cavern on the shores of an underground loch, Loch Malcolm. Verne writes with authority on mining activity but had never visited a Scottish mine. He declined such an opportunity at Oakley due to shortage of time and his material is gained from assiduous reading and a visit to the Anzin coal-mining district of northern France. If he writes convincingly on the technology and organisation of mining, he is less than accurate in his appreciation of geology of Central Scotland. In locating his coalfield close to Aberfoyle, Verne chose a geologically impossible location for mining. It is intriguing to pose the question as to why Verne, who had seen active coal mining in western Fife, should have chosen to situate the action at the foot of the Trossachs, knowing full well that this was geological nonsense. The reader will have no difficulty answering this poser for Verne required specific qualities of landscape and atmosphere for his tale. He needed a landscape of mystery and threat, where the existence of supernatural beings was credible. Moreover, he specifically needed a large loch, which after shattering earth movements would convulsively drain into the mine. As we have noted, the

Trossachs and Loch Katrine had left an indelible impression on Verne and provided him with a perfect setting for the combination of mineral, water and the supernatural his story required. Without revealing the details of the plot, the novel can be described as an ingenious blend of the real, the imaginary and the fantastic, enacted above and below ground, in darkness and in daylight and on land and water. If the presence of the supernatural is never distant, the characters in the novel are never less than solid and conform to what Verne perceived as demonstrating the endearing and enduring qualities of the Scot. The former manager, James Starr, who retired to Edinburgh on the closure of the mine, is portrayed as being a highly esteemed but not arrogant gentleman, a pillar of Edinburgh's scientific community but at the same time most at ease when associating with his loyal miners. Simon Ford and his son Harry, former miners who continued to live underground after the closure, are depicted as being physically and morally strong, doers rather than dreamers and clinging to the idea that the mine still had riches to be revealed and that its past glory could be re-found. Simon's wife, Madge, is seen to be calm, practical, warm hearted and a fierce guardian of harmony in the Ford household. As compared with these dogged characters, Harry's friend, Jack Ryan, is fey, a poet, singer and musician. He is a free spirit who brings a touch of lightness to the most sombre circumstances. Nell, the 'child of the cavern', is a young girl discovered abandoned and close to death deep underground. She is by no means a pathetic child but an intelligent, strong-minded girl, who under Madge's guidance rapidly becomes a young woman and a suitable wife for Harry. Finally, Silfax, Nell's great-grandfather, who has kept her underground all her life, emerges late in the plot as the perpetrator of the supposed supernatural events that punctuate the story. An aged, demented man, he regards the mine as his own and has done his best to drive out the population from Coal City and above all, to prevent the wedding of Nell and Harry. We should not forget a further 'personality', a giant Snowy Owl which plays a crucial role in the climax of the novel. Even as the story finishes with a happy ending, the Snowy Owl is to be observed flitting menacingly above the waters of Loch Malcolm.

The Underground City is thus a dichotomous novel in which half of the action takes place underground, often in darkness, and half above ground, where Verne exploits to the full his experiences from his 1859 visit. Thus the underground sequences give full range to his imaginative powers, whereas above ground he recycles his own journey down to the detail of names of steamers, railway lines and hotels. The description of the view from Arthur's Seat is repeated word for word from his travelogue, as is the experience of the steamer journey up Loch Lomond.

The success of The Underground City may be attributed to its multifaceted character. The book can be interpreted, more or less validly, in so many different ways. At a superficial level it might be regarded as a thriller in which as the plot unfolds, the atmosphere of menace and fear builds up to a dramatic crescendo. At a rather less superficial level it can be regarded as a romance in which many manifestations of love are portrayed – the love of Madge for her family, the affection between James Starr and the Fords, the fond nostalgia for the olden days of a strong mining community, the love of music and song on the part of Jack Ryan, the love expressed in the descriptions of mountains and lochs, the romantic love between Nell and Harry, and underlying all this, the love felt by Verne for 'his' Scotland. At the level of literary criticism, the novel may be regarded as being allegorical, and particularly an interplay of opposites. Within the vast 'womb' of the cavern, people live their lives in semi-darkness, in a constant temperature, protected from the outside world and nourished with coal by their geological mother. The story is a triumph of opposites, of dark and light, day and night, good and evil, love and hate and rational and supernatural. Yet another dimension is that of social and political commentary. Verne poses the possibility of an alternative lifestyle, a subterranean utopian existence lived in by people living and working for a common cause, in a relatively classless society and lacking the strife and tension of life on the earth's surface. In this sense, the novel lacks reference to the existence in nineteenth century Scottish mines of child and female labour, a horrific accident rate and incidence of chronic ill health and illiteracy. Verne was aware that at this time mineworkers suffered a virtual slave system but the story makes no mention of this and even the owners of New Aberfoyle are not referred to. Just as Verne calmly overlooked the fact that in the creation of the 'English' empire that he so disdained, many of the explorers, entrepreneurs, missionaries, military leaders and shipping magnates that underpinned the imperial endeavour were Scottish, so in *The Underground City* the cruel exploitation, the back-breaking and dangerous work, the poverty-stricken existence, are suppressed in favour of an image of contented family life, a high work ethic and a coherent non-radical society.

Verne paints for us a picture that combines the real world based on his own experience and research, and an imaginary world unconstrained by banal facts. If, for reasons of the plot, New Aberfoyle should be located irrationally, then so be it. Would the story have succeeded so vividly in a more mundane but geologically correct setting, for example between Stirling and Alloa? One must doubt it. Verne needed to exploit the part of Scotland that had most stirred his imagination in 1859.

Jules Verne was born in 1828 in Nantes, and died in March 1905. The year of publication of this translation thus marks the centenary of his death, which will be celebrated world wide including a plethora of new books. It is fitting that one of these commemorative works should be a book set in Scotland and published in Edinburgh, his favourite Scottish city – a fitting dedication to an extraordinary author who deserves to be better known in Scotland.

Professor Ian Thompson

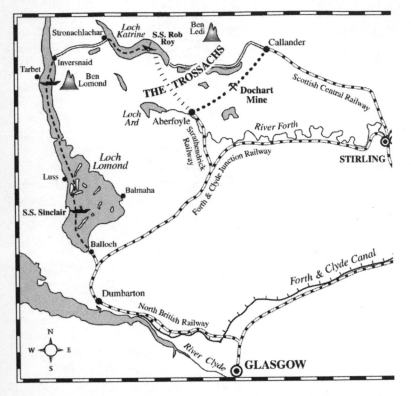

Map illustrating the action in The Underground City, nearly identical to the journey taken by Jules Verne through Scotland in 1859.

Map provided by Mike Shand, Department of Geography and Geomatics, University of Glasgow.

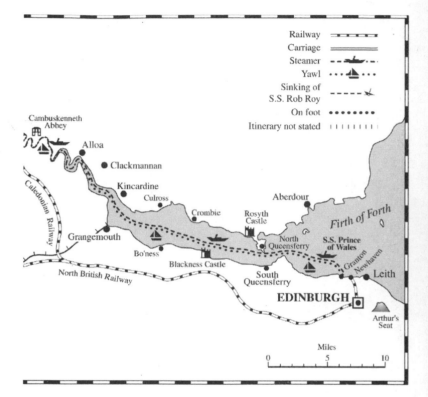

Railway
Carriage
Steamer
Yawl
Sinking of
S.S. Rob Roy
On foot
Itinerary not stated

Cambuskenneth
Abbey
Alloa
Clackmannan
Kincardine
Culross
Crombie
Rosyth
Castle
Aberdour
Firth of Forth
Caledonian Railway
Grangemouth
Bo'ness
North
Queensferry
S.S. Prince
of Wales
Granton
Newhaven
Leith
Blackness Castle
South
Queensferry
North British Railway
EDINBURGH
Arthur's
Seat

Miles
0   5   10

The Underground City

CHAPTER ONE

Two Contradictory Letters

Mr J R Starr, Engineer
30 Canongate
Edinburgh

If Mr James Starr will come tomorrow to the Yarrow
Shaft, Dochart Pit, Aberfoyle coalmines, he will be given
information of interest to him.
Mr James Starr will be awaited all day at Callander
station by Harry Ford, son of the former overman Simon
Ford.
He is requested to keep this invitation secret.

Such was the letter which James Starr received by the first post
on the 3rd December 18—, a letter which bore the postmark of
Aberfoyle, in Stirlingshire, Scotland.

The engineer's curiosity was sharply awakened. It did not
even occur to him that this letter might be a practical joke. He
had long known Simon Ford, one of the old foremen of the
Aberfoyle coalmines, of which for twenty years he, James Starr,
had been the general manager – what in British coalmines is
known as the 'viewer'.

James Starr was a solidly built man, who bore his fifty-five
years lightly; he could have passed for forty. He came from an
old Edinburgh family, and was one of its most distinguished
members. His work did credit to the worthy profession of engineers who gradually consume the coal-bearing underground of
the United Kingdom, in the Lowlands of Scotland as in Cardiff
and Newcastle. But, it was most particularly at the bottom of

these mysterious coalmines of Aberfoyle, which border the mines of Alloa and cover part of Stirlingshire, that the name of Starr had won general esteem. He had spent almost all of his life there. Among other things, Starr was a member of the Society of Antiquaries of Scotland, of which he had been appointed President. He was also one of the most active members of the Royal Institution, and the *Edinburgh Review* frequently published remarkable articles in his name. He was, manifestly, one of those wise, practical men to whom the United Kingdom owes its prosperity. He held high rank in Scotland's ancient capital, which, not only physically but even more so from a moral standpoint, was worthy of the title 'The Athens of the North'.

The British have given the entirety of their vast coalmines a most significant name. They call them, very aptly, the 'Black Indies', and these Indies have possibly made a greater contribution to increasing the surprising wealth of the United Kingdom than have the East Indies. For there a whole population of miners works day and night to extract coal – that precious fuel and vital element of industrial life – from beneath the British landscape.

At that time, specialists estimated the exhaustion of the coalfields to be in the distant future, and there was no fear of shortage in the short-term. There were still the coalmines of two worlds to be exploited. The factories, adapted to so many different purposes – locomotives, steam engines, steamers, gasworks, etc – were not about to run out of coal. Yet consumption had increased to such an extent these last years that certain layers had been exhausted up to their most meagre seams. Now abandoned, these mines left a useless complex of holed and furrowed land around their neglected shafts and deserted tunnels.

Such was precisely the case with the Aberfoyle mines.

Ten years previously, the last tub had raised the last ton of coal from the mine. The 'pit-face'[1] equipment, machines for

---

[1] The exploitation of a mine is divided between 'pit-face' work and 'surface' work; the former is carried out inside, the latter outside.

mechanical haulage on tunnel rails, trucks that formed the subterranean trains, underground trams, cage-lifts serving the production shafts, pipes whose compressed air operated the drills – in short, everything that made up the operating equipment had been taken out from the depths of the pits and abandoned above ground. The exhausted mine was like the body of a fantastically-proportioned mastodon whose various vital organs had been removed, leaving only the skeleton.

Of this equipment, there remained only the long wooden ladders that served the depths of the mine via the Yarrow shaft – the only one that, since the suspension of operations, still gave access to the lower tunnels of Dochart Pit.

Outside, the buildings that had previously housed the 'surface' work still showed the place where the shafts of the aforementioned pit had been sunk. It was completely abandoned, like all the other pits that together constituted the Aberfoyle coalmines.

It had been a sad day when, for the last time, the miners left the mine in which they had lived for so many years.

The engineer James Starr had gathered together the several thousand workers who made up the active and courageous population of the colliery. Pickers, putters, drivers, loaders, timbermen, roadmen, receivers, tippers, blacksmiths, carpenters, everyone – women, children, old people, pit-face and surface workers – was assembled in the huge courtyard of Dochart Pit, which had once overflowed with coal.

These good people, who would be scattered by the necessities of existence – who for long years had been succeeded father by son in old Aberfoyle – awaited the last farewells of the engineer before leaving for good. As a token of gratitude, the Company had shared out the profits of the previous year among them. Not much, in truth, for the yield from the seams had scarcely covered the operating costs; but enough to enable them to get by until they were taken on either in a neighbouring colliery or in one of the county's farms or factories.

James Starr held himself upright in front of the door of the vast lean-to under which the production shafts' powerful steam-powered machines had operated for so long.

Simon Ford, overman of Dochart Pit, then fifty-five years old, and several other works managers were around him.

James Starr uncovered his head. The miners, hats down, maintained a deep silence.

This farewell scene was touching, yet maintained a certain grandeur.

'Friends,' said the engineer, 'the moment to part has come. The Aberfoyle coalmines, which, for so many years, united us in a common endeavour, have now been exhausted. Our exploratory research has not led us to the discovery of a new seam, and the last lump of coal has been extracted from Dochart Pit!'

And, on saying this, James Starr indicated to the miners a block of coal that had been kept at the bottom of a tub.

'This lump of coal, my friends,' continued James Starr, 'is like the last drop of blood which ran through the veins of the colliery! We shall keep it, just as we have kept the first piece of carbon extracted from the Aberfoyle mines one hundred and fifty years ago. Between these two lumps, many generations of workers have followed one another into our pits. Now it has come to an end! These last words which your engineer addresses to you are words of farewell. You have lived from the mine, which has been emptied by your hand. The work was hard, but not without reward for you. Our great family will disperse, and it is unlikely that the future will ever reunite its scattered members. But do not forget that we have lived long together, and that for the miners of Aberfoyle, helping one another is a duty. Your former bosses will not forget that either. When we have worked together, we can no longer be strangers one to another. We will watch over you, and wherever you go as honest men, our recommendations will follow you. Farewell then, my friends, and may Heaven help you!'

4

That said, James Starr took into his arms the oldest workman of the mine, whose eyes were wet with tears. Then, the overmen from the various pits came to shake the engineer's hand, while the miners waved their hats and cried:

'Farewell, James Starr, our master and our friend!'

These goodbyes must have left an undying memory in all these brave hearts. But, gradually, as it must, this population sadly left the great yard. Emptiness surrounded James Starr. The black ground of the paths leading to Dochart Pit resounded one last time under the miners' feet, and then this noisy activity that had until then filled the Aberfoyle coalfield was followed by silence.

One man alone had stayed near James Starr.

It was the overman, Simon Ford. Near him was a young boy of fifteen, his son Harry, who had for a few years already been employed at the pit-face.

James Starr and Simon Ford knew each other, and in knowing each other, shared a mutual respect.

'Goodbye, Simon', said the engineer.

'Goodbye, Mr James,' replied the overman, 'or rather, let me say: until the next time.'

'Yes, until the next time, Simon!' repeated Starr. 'You know that I will always be happy to see you again, and to be able to speak to you about the past times of our old Aberfoyle!'

'I know, Mr James.'

'You are always welcome at my Edinburgh house.'

'Edinburgh is far!' replied the overman, shaking his head. 'Yes! Far from Dochart Pit.'

'Far, Simon? Where do you intend to live?'

'Right here, Mr James! We won't abandon the mine, our old wet nurse, just because her milk has dried up! My wife, my son and I, we will arrange things to stay faithful to her!'

'Then it is goodbye, Simon', replied the engineer, whose voice, despite himself, betrayed his emotion.

'No, I repeat: until the next time, Mr James!' replied the

James Starr

overman, 'On the word of Simon Ford, you will see Aberfoyle again!'

The engineer did not want to remove this last illusion from the overman. He embraced young Harry, who looked at him with large, emotional eyes. He shook Simon Ford's hand one last time and left the colliery for good.

That is what had happened ten years earlier; but despite the desire that the overman had expressed to see him again, Starr had heard nothing more about him.

And it was after ten years of separation that this letter from Simon Ford had arrived, inviting him to go to the old Aberfoyle coalmines without delay.

Information of interest to him – what could it be? Dochart Pit, Yarrow Shaft! What memories these names recalled to his mind! Yes! It had been a good time, one of work, of struggle – the best time in his engineering life!

James Starr reread the letter. He considered it from every angle. He was sorry, in truth, that Simon Ford had not added another line. He rather resented the fact that he had been so terse.

So perhaps the old overman had discovered a new seam to exploit? No!

James Starr recalled the painstaking care with which the Aberfoyle coalmines had been explored before the definitive cessation of operations. He himself had carried out the last surveys without finding any new deposit in this ground, ruined by over-exploitation. They had even tried to go back over the coal-bearing ground below the layers that are usually beneath it, such as the red Devonian sandstone, but without result. James Starr had thus abandoned the mine with the absolute conviction that it no longer contained any vestige of fuel.

'No,' he repeated to himself, 'No! How could it be possible that something that escaped my exploration could have been found by Simon Ford? Yet, the old overman must be well aware that only one thing in the world could interest me – and this

invitation, which I have to keep secret, to go to Dochart Pit...'
James Starr kept coming back to that.

Moreover, the engineer knew Simon Ford to be a skilful
miner, particularly gifted in the instinct of the trade. He had not
seen him again since the operations at Aberfoyle had ceased.
He did even know what had become of the old overman.
He could not say what he was doing, or even where he was
staying with his wife and son. All he knew was that the appointment had been given for the Yarrow Shaft, and that Harry,
Simon Ford's son, would be waiting for him at Callander Station
all of the following day. It clearly, therefore, involved visiting
Dochart Pit.

'I shall go, I shall go!' said James Starr, who felt his excitement rise as the hour approached.

This worthy engineer was one of those passionate individu-
als whose brain is constantly overheated like a kettle on the hob.
Not a gently simmering one, but one in which ideas spurt and
steam. Now, on this day, the ideas of James Starr were boiling
furiously.

But then a very unexpected thing happened, like a dousing of
cold water on his brain.

At about six in the evening, by the third post, James Starr's
maid brought a second letter.
This letter was enclosed in a rough envelope, the address of
which indicated a hand little practised in the use of the pen.

James Starr ripped open the envelope. It contained a mere
scrap of paper, yellowed with time, which appeared to have been
torn from some old, discarded notebook.

On the paper was just one sentence:

'There is no point in James Starr troubling himself – the
letter of Simon Ford is now irrelevant.'

And no signature.

CHAPTER TWO

On the Road

JAMES STARR'S TRAIN of thought came to an abrupt halt as soon as he had read this second letter, contradicting the first.

'What can it mean?' he wondered.

He picked up the half-torn envelope again. Like the other, it bore the Aberfoyle postmark. It had therefore come from the same part of Stirlingshire. The old miner had obviously not written it. But, no less obviously, the author of the second letter knew the overman's secret, because it formally annulled the invitation given to the engineer to come to the Yarrow Shaft.

So was it true that the first communication was now irrelevant? Did someone want to prevent James Starr from bothering himself, whether pointlessly or not? Was there not rather a malevolent intention in it to thwart Simon Ford's projects?

That was what James Starr concluded after careful reflection. The contradiction between the two letters only made him all the more determined to go to Dochart Pit. Besides, if all this was just a practical joke, better to make sure of it. But James Starr was inclined to attach more credence to the first letter than to the second – that is to say to the request of a man such as Simon Ford rather than to the opinion of an anonymous contradictor.

'In truth, the fact that someone is trying to influence my decision means that Simon Ford's message must be of extreme importance! Tomorrow, I shall be at the designated meeting-place at the appointed hour!'

As it was now evening, James Starr prepared for his departure. Since it was possible that his absence would be prolonged for several days, he wrote to Sir W Elphiston, President of the Royal Institution, that he would be unable to attend the next meeting of the Society. He also disengaged himself from two or

Harry

three business matters, which should have occupied him during the week. Then, having instructed his maid to prepare a travelling bag, he went to bed, more excited by the matter than was, perhaps, merited.

The next day at five o'clock, James Starr leaped out of bed, got dressed in warm clothes – for it was cold and wet – and left his house in the Canongate to catch the steamboat at Granton Pier, which goes up the Forth to Stirling in three hours.

Perhaps for the first time on crossing the Canongate[2], James Starr did not turn round to look at Holyrood, the palace of the old sovereigns of Scotland. He did not notice the guards in front of its gates, dressed in the traditional Scottish costume of green kilts, tartan plaid and a long-haired goatskin sporran. Although he was a great fan of Walter Scott, as is every true son of Caledonia, the engineer failed to glance as usual at the inn where Waverley stayed and in which the tailor had brought him his famous tartan war costume, the one which the widow Flockart had so naively admired. Neither did he acknowledge the little square where the Highlanders had discharged their guns, endangering the life of Flora MacIvor, after the Pretender's victory. The desolate dial of the prison clock extended to the middle of the street: he looked at it only to make sure that he would not be late for the departure. Nor did he glance at the house of the great reformer John Knox, in Netherbow Lane, the only man who could not be seduced by Mary Stuart's smiles. But, taking the busy High Street, which is so intricately described in the novel *The Abbot*, he hurried towards the Bridges, which link the three ridges of Edinburgh.

A few minutes later, James Starr arrived at the General Railway station, and the train departed half an hour later for Newhaven, an attractive fishing village situated a mile from Leith, Edinburgh's port. The tide was then rising over the blackish and rocky beach of the coast. The first waves washed the landing-stage, a sort of jetty supported by chains. On the left,

[2] Principal and famous street of Edinburgh's Old Town.

one of the boats that served the Forth between Edinburgh and Stirling was moored at Granton Pier.

At that moment, the chimney of the *Prince of Wales* spewed out swirls of black smoke, and its steam-engine snored deafeningly. At the sound of the clock, which struck just a few times, the late voyagers hurried over. They were a crowd of merchants, farmers and ministers, these last recognisable by their short trousers, long frock-coats, and white dog-collars.

James Starr was certainly not the last to embark. He jumped nimbly on to the *Prince of Wales*' gangway. Although it was pouring with rain, not one of the passengers thought of seeking shelter in the steamboat's lounge. Everyone stayed where they were, wrapped in their travelling clothes, some reviving themselves now and again with the gin or whisky from their hip-flask – what they call 'warming up the insides'. The clock struck its final chime, the moorings were cast off, and the *Prince of Wales* manoeuvred to leave the little dock that was sheltering it from the waves of the North Sea.

The Firth of Forth is the deep gulf between the banks of the county of Fife to the north, and those of Linlithgow, Edinburgh and Haddington to the south. It forms the Forth estuary, a river of little importance – a sort of deep-water Thames or Mersey – which descends from the western flanks of Ben Lomond and flows into the sea at Kincardine.

It would be just a short trip, from Granton Pier to the end of the estuary, if there were not the need for numerous detours to stop at the various ports of call of the two banks. Towns, villages and cottages spread along the banks of the Forth between the trees and the fertile countryside. James Starr, sheltered under the large gangway that stretched out between the paddle boxes, was not looking at any of this landscape, now hatched with fine rain. He was more concerned that he had not attracted the special attention of any passenger. For perhaps the anonymous author of the second letter was on the boat. However, the engineer was unable to intercept any suspicious look.

On leaving Granton Pier the *Prince of Wales* headed for the narrow straits between the two points of South Queensferry and North Queensferry. There the Forth forms a deep waterway where ships of a hundred tons can navigate. Through the brief bright intervals in the surrounding mists the snowy summits of the Grampian hills could be glimpsed.

Soon the steamboat lost sight of the village of Aberdour, of Inchcolm island, crowned by the ruins of a seventeenth-century abbey, of the remains of Barnbougle Castle, then of Donibristle, where the son-in-law of Regent Murray had been assassinated, and of the islet of Garvie. It crossed the strait of Queensferry, leaving Rosyth Castle on the left, where once had lived a branch of the Stuarts linked to Cromwell's mother, passing by Blackness Castle, still fortified in accordance with one of the articles of the treaty of the Union, and alongside the quays of the little port of Charleston, from where the lime of Lord Elgin's quarries is exported.

The weather was very bad. Bellowing gusts that came like whirlwinds flung forth sprays of stinging rain.

James Starr was not a little anxious. Would Harry Ford's son keep the appointment? From experience he knew that miners, used to the deep calm of the mines, braved these great turbulences of the atmosphere rather less willingly than factory-workers or labourers. It was a good four miles from Callander to Dochart Pit and the Yarrow Shaft. That might, to some extent, make the old overman's son late. Nevertheless, the engineer was more preoccupied by the thought that the meeting given in the first letter had been cancelled by the second. That was, if truth be told, his greatest concern.

In any case, if Harry Ford was not there at the arrival of the Callander train, James Starr was determined to go to Dochart Pit alone, and even, if necessary, as far as the village of Aberfoyle. There he would surely obtain news of Simon Ford, and would find out where the old overman currently resided.

Meanwhile, the *Prince of Wales* continued to raise big waves under the force of its paddlewheels. Nothing of the two banks could be seen, nor of the villages of Crombie, Torryburn, Newmills, Carriden House, Kirkgrange, nor Salt-Pans on the right. The little port of Bo'ness and the port of Grangemouth, excavated in the mouth of the Forth-Clyde canal, disappeared in the damp fog. Culross, the old borough and the ruins of its Cistercian Abbey, Kincardine and its building yard, where the steamboat made stops, Airth Castle and its square, eighteenth century tower, Clackmannan and its castle, taken by Robert the Bruce, were not even visible through the heavy streaks of rain.

The *Prince of Wales* stopped at Alloa pier to drop off some passengers. James Starr felt his heart twinge as, after ten years of absence, he passed by this little town, the site of operations for the important collieries that still fed a large population of workers. His imagination took him underground, where the miners' picks were still digging to great profit. The Alloa mines, which nearly touched those of Aberfoyle, continued to enrich the county, while the neighbouring seams, exhausted so many years ago, had not one single labourer!

On leaving Alloa the steamboat sailed on through the numerous meanderings that the Forth makes over a distance of nineteen miles. It navigated easily between the tall trees of the two banks. In a bright spell appeared momentarily the ruins of Cambuskenneth Abbey, which dates from the seventeenth century. Then there was Stirling Castle, and the royal borough of the same name, where the Forth, crossed by two bridges, is no longer navigable by tall-masted boats.

The *Prince of Wales* had hardly docked when James Starr stepped sprightly onto the quay. Five minutes later he reached Stirling station. An hour later, he was getting off the train at Callander, a large village on the left bank of the Teith.

There, in front of the station, was a young man, who at once approached the engineer.

It was Harry, the son of Simon Ford.

CHAPTER THREE

Beneath the United Kingdom

TO UNDERSTAND THIS tale, it is worth briefly recalling the origin of coal.

During geological epochs, when the terrestrial sphere was still in the process of formation, a thick atmosphere enveloped it, completely saturated with water vapour and widely impregnated with carbonic acid. These vapours gradually condensed into flooding downpours, which fell as if they had been sprayed from the necks of several millions of billions of bottles of Seltzer water. It was, in fact, a liquid full of carbonic acid, which fell torrentially on a pasty, unconsolidated ground, subject to sudden and gradual deformations, kept in this semi-fluid state as much by the massive internal flames as by the fires of the sun. The internal heat had not yet been stored up at the centre of the globe. The Earth's crust, thin and not fully hardened, let it seep out through its pores. From this grew a phenomenal vegetation – such as is no doubt produced on the surface of the lesser planets Venus or Mercury, which are closer than the Earth to the radiant sun.

The still unstable floor of the continents was covered by huge forests; carbonic acid, so suitable for the development of the vegetable kingdom, was abundant. Thus, the vegetation developed in tree-form. There was not one single herbaceous plant. Everywhere were enormous clumps of monotonous trees, without flowers or fruit, which could not sufficiently nourish any living creature. The Earth was not yet ready for the arrival of the animal kingdom.

These antediluvian forests were composed as follows: the dominant species of cryptogame vasculars; calamites – varieties of horsetail trees; lepidodendrons – sorts of giant lycopodes, twenty-five or thirty metres high, one metre wide at their base; asterophylles; ferns; gigantically-proportioned sigillaries, the imprints of which are found in the mines of Saint Etienne – all imposing plants, the like of which we do not find among the humbler specimens of the habitable Earth. Such were the plants – little varied in species, but enormous in their development – which exclusively made up the forests of that period.

At that time these trees were drowning with their roots in a sort of immense lagoon, profoundly saturated from the mix of fresh and salt water. They avidly assimilated carbon, which they gradually extracted from an atmosphere still unsuited to the functions of life, and it could be said that it was their destiny to store it up as coal, in the very bowels of the globe.

It was the period of earthquakes and tectonic movements, caused by internal revolutions and deap-seated action, which suddenly changed the still uncertain alignments of the Earth's surface. Here, intumescences would become mountains; there, the abysses to be filled by the oceans and seas. And so, entire forests were pushed into the Earth's crust, through the moving beds, until they found something to push against, such as a primitive basement of granitic rocks, or by piling up they formed a resistant mass.

In the bowels of the Earth, the geological structure is as follows: the Primary rocks, which is overlain by the sedimentary material, composed of the eroded Primary layer; then the Secondary layer of which the coal deposits occupy the lower level; then the Tertiary terrains, and above them, the deposits of ancient and modern alluvials.

At this period, the waters – which as yet were not contained in beds, and which were created by condensation at all the corners of the globe – flowed in torrents, tearing from the barely formed rocks the material that was to become shale, sandstone and limestone. They settled on top of the peaty forests, depositing the elements of the layers that would form above the coal. With time – the passing of millions of years – these terrains

Gigantically-proportioned sigillaries...

hardened, formed layers and enclosed the whole mass of sunken forests under a thick shell of pudding-stone, shale, compact or crumbly sandstone, gravel and pebbles.

What happened in this gigantic crucible, where the accumulated vegetable matter was pushed down to variable depths? A veritable chemical reaction – a kind of distillation. All the carbon contained in the plants collected, and coal gradually formed under the dual influence of extreme pressure and the high temperature of the internal fires, which raged so close at this time.

Thus one kingdom replaced another in this slow but irresistible reaction. The vegetable was transformed into mineral. All these plants, which had lived a vegetable life with the active sap of the beginning, petrified. A few of the substances enclosed in this vast herbarium, not completely deformed, left their fossil imprints on other products more quickly mineralised, which squeezed them like a hydraulic press, with an incalculable pressure. At the same time, shells and zoophytes from star-fish, polyparies and spiriferes to fish and lizards, brought by the waters, left clear impressions cleanly printed on the still-soft coal.[3]

Pressure seems to have played a considerable role in the formation of the carboniferous deposits. Indeed, the various types of coal which industry uses are due to its degree of power. Thus, anthracite is found at the lowest layers of coal-bearing ground, which, being almost entirely without volatile material contains the largest quantity of carbon. At the highest layers, conversely, is lignite and fossilised wood, substances in which the amount of carbon is considerably less. Between these two layers, we find, according to the degree of pressure to which they have been subjected, seams of graphite, fat or lean coal. We can even

---

[3] It should, moreover, be noted that all these plants, of which impressions have been found belong to species found today only in the equatorial zones of the globe. We can therefore conclude that at this period, the heat was the same all over the Earth. Either it was brought by warm currents, or the internal fires were felt at its surface through a porous crust. Thus is the formation of coal-bearing deposits beneath all the terrestrial latitudes explained.

confirm that it is because of a lack pressure that the peat-bog layer has not been completely transformed.

In summary, the origin of the coalmines, in whichever corner of the globe, is as follows: the engulfing of the large forests of the geological period into the Earth's crust, then, with time, the mineralisation of the plants under the conditions of pressure and heat, and in reaction to the carbonic acid.

However, Nature, normally so extravagant, did not bury enough forests for a consumption of several thousand years. Coal will run out one day – that much is certain. So a forced idleness will impose itself on the entire world's machinery, unless some new fuel replaces carbon. At a period more or less far off, there will be no more coal seams, apart from those covered by a permanent layer of ice in Greenland near the Baffin Sea, the exploitation of which is near impossible. That is the inevitable fate. The still lavishly rich coal basins of America – of Salt Lake, Oregon and California – will one day have an insufficient yield. Such will also be the case with the coalmines of Cape Breton and Saint Lawrence, the deposits of Allegheny, Pennsylvania, Virginia, Illinois, Indiana and Missouri. Although the carboniferous beds of North America might be ten times more considerable than the entire world's deposits combined, before a hundred centuries pass the industrial monster of a million mouths will have devoured the last lump of the world's coal.

The scarcity, it is understood, will be felt more quickly in the Old World. While there exist layers of combustible mineral in Abyssinia, Natal, Zambeze, Mozambique and Madagascar, their regular exploitation presents the greatest difficulties. Those of Burma, China, Cochin China, Japan and Central Asia will be exhausted fairly quickly. The British will almost certainly empty Australia of coal products, relatively abundantly buried in its ground, before the day the United Kingdom itself lacks coal. Already by this period, the carbon-bearing seams of Europe, pursued until their last veins, will have been abandoned.

We may estimate the amounts of coal that have been consumed since the discovery of the first deposits with the following figures: the coal basins of Russia, Saxony and Bavaria comprise six hundred thousand hectares; those of Spain, one hundred and fifty thousand; those of Bohemia and Austria, one hundred and fifty thousand. The basins of Belgium, forty leagues long, three wide, also add up to one hundred and fifty thousand hectares, which extend under the territories of Liège, Namur, Mons, and Charleroi. In France, the basin between the Loire and the Rhône, Rive-de-Gier, Saint-Etienne, Givors, Epinac, Blanzy, le Creuzot; the operations at Gard, Alais, Grand-Combe; those from Aveyron to Aubin; the seams of Carmaux, Brassac, Graissessac; and in the north, Anzin, Valenciennes, Lens, Béthune cover around three hundred and fifty thousand hectares.

The country the richest in coal, is incontestably the United Kingdom. With the exception of Ireland, which is almost entirely lacking in combustible material, it possesses enormous carboniferous resources – which like all resources are finite. Newcastle, the most important of these various basins, which lies beneath the county of Northumberland, produces up to thirty million tons annually, that is to say nearly a third of British consumption, and more than double the French production. The Welsh basin, which has concentrated an entire population of miners in Cardiff, Swansea, and Newport, yields annually ten million tons of the highly prized coal that bears its name. In the midlands, the basins of the counties of York, Lancaster, Derby, Stafford are exploited – less productive, but still with a considerable yield. Finally, in the part of Scotland between Edinburgh and Glasgow, between the two seas that cut in so deeply, is one of the most immense coalfields of the United Kingdom. The various basins total no less than sixteen thousand hectares, and produce annually up to one hundred million tons of black fuel.

But what does it matter? Consumption will increase, through the needs of industry and commerce, so that these resources will be used up. We will not reach the third millennium since Christ before the miner's hand has emptied, throughout Europe, these warehouses in which, to continue a fitting metaphor, the sun's heat from the earliest days is stored.[4]

Now, precisely at the time when this story was taking place, one of the most important coalmines of the Scottish basin had been exhausted by over-rapid exploitation. Indeed, it was in this region between Edinburgh and Glasgow, over an average width of ten to twelve miles, that the Aberfoyle mines lay, where the engineer James Starr had for so long directed the operations.

For ten years earlier, these mines had had to be abandoned. New seams were not to be found, despite surveys that had been carried out at a depth of up to fifteen hundred, even two thousand feet, and when James Starr left, it was with the conviction that the most meagre seam had been exploited to complete exhaustion.

It was, therefore, more than plain that, under such conditions, the discovery of a new coal basin in the depths of subterranean Britain would have been a considerable event. Would the information heralded by Simon Ford report something of this nature? That is what James Starr was wondering, that is what he hoped.

Was he, in short, being summoned to make a new conquest of another corner of these rich Black Indies? He wanted to believe so.

The second letter had momentarily derailed his ideas on the subject, but now he did not give it a second thought. Moreover, the old overman's son was there, waiting for him at the appointed meeting place. The anonymous letter was, therefore, no longer of any consequence.

---

[4] Taking the progression of the consumption of coal into account, these are the latest estimates:

France... in 1,140 years

Britain	800
Belguim	750
Germany	300

In America, because of an annual 500 million tons, the coalfields could produce coal for 6,000 years.

The instant the engineer put his foot on the platform, the young man approached him.

'Are you Harry Ford?' James Starr asked excitedly, without any other introduction.

'Yes, Mr Starr.'

'I would not have recognised you, my boy! Ah! It is because, in ten years, you have become a man!'

'I recognised you,' replied the young miner, who was holding his hat in his hand. 'You haven't changed, sir. You are the man who embraced me on the day of farewell at Dochart Pit. One doesn't forget that kind of thing!'

'Put your hat on, Harry,' said the engineer. 'It is pouring with rain, and politeness should not extend to catching cold.'

'Shall we take shelter, Mr Starr?' asked Harry Ford.

'No, Harry. The weather has set in. It will rain all day, and I am in a hurry. Let's go.'

'As you wish,' replied the young man.

'Tell me, Harry, is your father well?'

'Very well, Mr Starr.'

'And your mother?'

'Her as well.'

'Was it your father that wrote to me, to give me the appointment at the Yarrow Shaft?'

'No, it was me.'

'But did Simon Ford then send me a second letter cancelling this meeting?' asked the engineer excitedly.

'No, Mr Starr,' replied the young miner.

'Well!' replied James Starr, without further mentioning the anonymous letter.

Then, taking up the conversation again, he asked:

'Can you tell me what old Simon wants with me?'

'My father has reserved the right to tell you himself, Mr Starr.'

'But you know what it is...?'

'I know what it is.'

'Well then, Harry, I shall not ask you any more. Let us go, though, for I am eager to speak to Simon Ford. Where does he live, by the way?' he asked.

'In the mine.'

'What! In Dochart Pit?'

'Yes, Mr Starr,' replied Harry Ford.

'What! Your family has not left the old mine since operations ceased?'

'Not one day, Mr Starr. You know my father. That's where he was born, that's where he'll die.'

'I can understand that, Harry... I can understand that. His native mine! He did not want to abandon it! And do you like it there?'

'Yes, Mr Starr,' replied the young miner, 'for we love each other fondly, and we have few needs.'

'Well, Harry,' said the engineer. 'Let's go!'

And James Starr, following the young man, began to cross the streets of Callander.

Ten minutes later, they had left the town.

CHAPTER FOUR

Dochart Pit

HARRY FORD WAS a tall lad of twenty-five, vigorous and well-built. He had a rather serious mien and a habitually pensive attitude, which had, since childhood, been remarked upon by his comrades in the mine. His regular features, his deep and soft eyes, his tousled hair, more brown than blonde, his natural charm, all combined to make the perfect Lowlander, that is to say, a superb specimen of the Scotsman of the plain. Hardened from the youngest age by work in the colliery, he was nonetheless a dependable companion, with a brave and good nature. Guided by his father and pushed by his own instincts, he had worked and learned early, so that at an age when most are barely apprentices, he had succeeded in making someone of himself – one of the first from his class – in a country that has few fools, since it does everything to suppress ignorance. If, during these first years of his adolescence, the pick had not left Harry Ford's hand, the young miner was nevertheless not slow in acquiring sufficient knowledge to rise up the hierarchy of the colliery, and he would certainly have succeeded his father as overman of Dochart Pit, had the mine not been abandoned.

James Starr was still a good walker, but he would not have followed his guide easily if the latter had not moderated his pace.

The rain was now falling less heavily. The large drops turned to spray before hitting the ground. It was more a wet wind that ran through the air, lifted up by a fresh breeze.

Harry Ford and James Starr – the young man carrying the engineer's light baggage – followed the left bank of the river for about a mile. After passing along its sinuous shore, they took a road that thrust inland under the tall, dripping trees. Vast pastures spread out on one side, and on the other, were isolated

The young man carrying the engineer's light baggage...

farms. Some herds were grazing peacefully on the lush green grass of these Scottish Lowland fields. They were hornless cattle, or young sheep with silky fleeces, which resembled children's toys. No shepherd was to be seen, sheltered as he doubtless was, in some hollow in a tree; but the collie, a dog particular to this region of the United Kingdom and renowned for its vigilance, was running around the pasture.

The Yarrow Shaft was about four miles from Callander. While he walked, James Starr could not help but be impressed. He had not seen the country since the day that last ton from the Aberfoyle mines had been emptied into the wagons of the Glasgow railway. Agricultural life now replaced the noisier and more active industrial life. The contrast was all the more striking, as during winter, the fields showed little sign of human activity. But in the past, in all seasons, the population of miners, above as below, brought life to the land. The great carts of coal passed day and night. The rails, now buried on their decayed sleepers, used to creak under the weight of wagons. Now, stone and dirt tracks were gradually replacing the operations' old railtracks. James Starr felt he was crossing a desert.

The engineer looked about him with a saddened eye. He stopped occasionally to recover his breath. He listened. The air had not thus far resounded with the faraway whistles and heaving din of machines. On the horizon there was not one of those blackish vapours that the industrial man loves to find mixed with the large clouds. No high cylindrical or square chimney spewed out smoke, after having been fed at the coal seam itself, no exhaust pipe gasped to blow out its white smoke. The ground, previously blackened with coal dust, had a clean appearance, to which James Starr's eyes were unaccustomed.

When the engineer stopped, Harry Ford stopped too. The young miner waited in silence. He was well aware of what was going on in the mind of his companion, and he keenly shared this impression, being himself a child of the mine, whose whole life had been spent in the depths of the ground.

The engineer looked about him with a saddened eye.

'Yes, Harry, all this has changed,' said James Starr. 'But the very fact of exploitation meant that the coal treasures had to run out one day! You miss those days?'

'I miss them, Mr Starr,' replied Harry. 'The work was hard, but it was rewarding, like every struggle.'

'Without doubt, my boy. The struggle of all those moments, the danger of roof-falls, fires, floods, firedamp explosions that strike like lightning! One had to be prepared for all those perils. You put it well! It was a struggle, and consequently, a stirring life!'

'The Alloa miners were more fortunate than the Aberfoyle miners, Mr Starr!'

'Yes, Harry,' replied the engineer.

'In truth,' cried the young man, 'it is a pity that the whole earthly globe were not made up solely of coal! There would have been enough for several million years!'

'No doubt, Harry, but you have to admit, however, that Nature has shown herself to have foresight in making our spheroid more principally of sandstone, limestone and granite, which cannot be consumed by fire!'

'Do you mean, Mr Starr, that mankind would have ended up burning its globe?'

'Yes! In its entirety, my boy,' replied the engineer. 'The Earth would have passed until its last lump into the furnaces of locomotives, steam engines, steamers, gasworks, and surely, that is how our world would have ended one fine day!'

'There is no fear of that, Mr Starr. But now, the coalmines will be exhausted, no doubt, more quickly than the statistics make out!'

'That will happen, Harry, and in my view, Britain is perhaps wrong to exchange her fuel for the gold of other nations.'

'Indeed,' replied Harry.

'I know well,' added the engineer, 'that neither hydraulic energy, nor electricity have had their last word, and that we will use these two forces more comprehensively one day. But even so! Coal is a very practical fuel and lends itself easily to the various needs of industry. Unfortunately, men cannot produce it by willpower! While the outside forests re-grow incessantly under the influence of heat and water, the interior forests do not replicate themselves, and the world will never again find the conditions desirable for them to do so!'

James Starr and his guide, while talking, had resumed their quick pace. An hour after leaving Callander, they reached Dochart Pit.

Even someone less involved would have been touched by the sad picture of the abandoned establishment. It was like the skeleton of a once living creature.

Over a vast area, bordered by some thin trees, the ground was still cloaked by the black dust of the combustible mineral, but neither grit, nor lumps, nor any fragment of coal was still to be seen. Everything had long since been removed and consumed.

Standing on a low hill was the silhouette of an enormous timber framework, which the ravishes of the sun and the rain were slowly eating away. At the top of the structure was a huge iron wheel, and lower down were the rounded forms of the huge drums on which once turned the cables that pulled up the cages to ground level.

At the lower level, you could see the housings for dilapidated machines where once the steel and copper mechanisms shone brightly. Some sections of wall were lying on the ground amid rotting joists, green with damp. There were the remains of balance wheels and the stem of the exhaust pumps, broken and crushed bearings, broken-toothed cogwheels, over-turned tipping engines, some steps fixed on trestles resembling large ichthyosaur bones, rails borne by some broken sleeper that two or three wobbly stilts still supported, tramways which would not have resisted the weight of an empty wagon. Such was the desolate sight of Dochart Pit.

The coping of the shaft, constructed in undressed stone, disappeared under thick moss. Here, you could see the vestiges of a cage, there the remains of a depot where the coal had been stocked for separation by quality and size. Finally, there was a tangled mass of containers with bits of chain, fragments of gigantic trestles, the casements of a ripped-open boiler, and twisted pistons, while long poles leant over the mouth of the pump shaft, gangways trembled in the wind with the poppies beside cracking walls, half-collapsed roofs beneath towering loose brick chimneys, which looked like those modern cannons with breeches strengthened by cylindrical rings. All this gave a sharp impression of abandon, of misery, of sadness, somehow different from the ruins of an old stone castle, or the remains of a dismantled fortress.

'It is devastation!' said James Starr, looking at the young man who did not reply.

The two went under the lean-to that covered the mouth of the Yarrow Shaft, which still had ladders giving access to the lower tunnels of the pit.

The engineer leant over the hole.

In the past the powerful breath of air inhaled by the ventilators had poured out from there. Now it was a silent abyss. It was like looking down the mouth of an extinct volcano.

James Starr and Harry stepped onto the first landing.

When it was in full production, ingenious engines served certain shafts of the Aberfoyle coalmines, which, in this respect, were perfectly equipped: cages fitted out with automatic parachute brakes, biting on the wooden runners; winding ladders, nicknamed 'enginemen', which by simple oscillation enabled the miners to descend without danger and to come up again without effort.

But these perfected contraptions had been removed since the end of operations. All that remained in the Yarrow Shaft was a long succession of ladders, separated by narrow landings of fifty-by-fifty feet. Thirty of these ladders, placed end to end, allowed descent to the floor of the lower tunnel, a depth of fifteen hundred feet. It was the sole means of communication that existed between the ground and the bottom of Dochart Pit.

All this gave a sharp impression of abandon...

As for the ventilation, it operated by the Yarrow Shaft, which the tunnels communicated with another shaft that opened at a higher level – the hot air moved out naturally through this sort of upside-down siphon.

'I will follow you, my boy,' said the engineer, indicating to the young man to go before him.

'As you wish, Mr Starr.'

'Do you have a lamp?'

'Yes, and how I wish that it were still the safety lamp which we used in the past!'

'Indeed,' replied James Starr, 'but firedamp explosions are no longer to be feared now!'

Harry was equipped with just a simple oil lamp, the wick of which he lit. In the coalmine, empty of coal, leaks of carburetted hydrogen gas could no longer occur. So, no explosion to fear, and no need to place between the flame and the ambient air the metallic grill that prevents gas from catching fire on the outside. The Davy lamp, the perfected solution to the problem, no longer had a purpose here. But if the danger did not exist, it was because its cause had disappeared and with it, the fuel that previously provided the wealth of Dochart Pit.

Harry descended the first rungs of the upper ladder. James Starr followed him. Soon both found themselves in a deep darkness broken only by the glow of the lamp. The young man lifted it above his head, better to light his companion.

The engineer and his guide climbed down a dozen ladders with that measured miner's step. They were still in good condition.

James Starr observed with curiosity what the faint glimmer allowed him to make out of the walls of the dark shafts, still covered with a half-rotten wooden lining.

On arriving at the fifteenth landing, that is to say half-way down, they stopped for a few moments.

'Decidedly, I do not have your legs, my boy,' said the engineer, breathing heavily, 'but even so, they still work!'

'You are sturdy, Mr Starr,' replied Harry, 'and you see, living for so long in the mine has its effect.'

'You are right, Harry. In the past, when I was twenty, I would have descended in one breath. Come on, let us go on!'

But just when the two of them were about to leave the landing, a voice, some way off, sounded in the depths of the shaft. It arrived like a sound wave, progressively swelling, and it became increasingly distinct.

'Hey! Who goes there?' asked the engineer, stopping Harry.

'I couldn't say,' replied the young miner.

'It is not your old father?'

'Him! No, Mr Starr.'

'Some neighbour then?'

'We don't have any neighbours at the bottom of the pit,' replied Harry 'We're alone, completely alone.'

'Well! Let's let this intruder pass,' said James Starr. 'Those who are going down should give way to those coming up.'

The two of them waited.

The voice resounded at that instant with a magnificent burst, as if carried by a vast acoustic sail, and shortly the lyrics of a Scottish song reached quite clearly the ears of the young miner.

'The song of the lochs!' cried Harry. 'Ah! I'll be surprised if it comes from a mouth other than Jack Ryan's.'

'And who is this Jack Ryan, who sings in such a fine fashion?' asked James Starr.

'An old comrade from the colliery,' replied Harry.

Then, leaning over the landing, he cried:

'Hey! Jack!'

'Is that you, Harry? Wait for me, I'm coming.'

And the song resumed louder still.

A few moments later, a tall lad of twenty-five, with a bright face, smiling eyes, a joyful mouth, and blazing blond hair, appeared at the bottom of the cone of light projected by his lantern, and he set foot on the landing of the fifteenth ladder.

The first thing he did was to shake vigorously the hand that

Harry had just extended to him.

'Delighted to see you again!' he cried. 'But, St Mungo protect me, if I had known that you were coming back up to ground today I would have saved myself the descent of the Yarrow Shaft!

'Mr James Starr,' said Harry at this point, turning his lamp towards the engineer, who had stayed in the shadows.

'Mr Starr!' replied Jack Ryan. 'Ah! The engineer, I wouldn't have recognised you, sir. Since I left the pit, my eyes are no longer accustomed to seeing in the dark.'

'And I remember now a little lad who was always singing. Now we are a good ten years on from then, my boy! No doubt it was you?'

'The very same, Mr Starr, and, in changing my trade, I haven't changed my humour, you see? Bah! Laughing and singing is better, I imagine, than crying and moaning!'

'Without doubt, Jack Ryan. And what do you do now, since leaving the mine?'

'I work at Melrose Farm, near Irvine, in Renfrewshire, forty miles from here. Ach! It's not as good as our Aberfoyle mines! The pick would go better in my hand than the spade or the goad! And then, in the old pit, there were sonorous corners, joyous echoes which cheerfully returned you your songs, whereas up there... But you are going to pay a visit to old Simon, then, Mr Starr?'

'Yes, Jack,' replied the engineer.

'Then don't let me keep you.'

'Tell me, Jack,' asked Harry, 'what brought you to the cottage today?'

'I wanted to see you, my friend,' replied Jack Ryan, 'and invite you to the Irvine clan festival. I'm the local piper,[5] you know! There will be singing and dancing!'

'Thank you, Jack, but I can't come.'

---

[5] The 'piper' is the bagpipe player in Scotland.

'You can't come?'

'Yes, Mr Starr's visit might be prolonged, and I have to take him back to Callander.'

'Harry, the Irvine clan festival isn't for eight days. I imagine that Mr Starr's visit will be over by then, and nothing will further detain you at the cottage!'

'Indeed, Harry,' replied James Starr, 'You should make the most of your friend Jack's invitation!'

'Well then, I accept, Jack,' said Harry. 'I'll see you at the Irvine festival in eight days.'

'In eight days, it's a date! Goodbye, Harry! Your servant, Mr Starr! I'm very glad to have seen you again! I'll be able to give your news to friends. Nobody has forgotten you, Mr Starr.'

'And likewise I have not forgotten anybody,' said James Starr.

'Thank you for everything, sir,' replied Jack Ryan.

'Goodbye, Jack!' said Harry, shaking his friend's hand one last time.

And Jack Ryan, resuming his song, soon disappeared into the heights of the shaft, dimly lit by his lamp.

A quarter of an hour later, James Starr and Harry descended the final ladder, and set foot on the last floor of the pit.

Around the roundabout that formed the bottom of the Yarrow Shaft extended various tunnels that had served in the exploitation of the last coal-bearing seam of the mine. They were bored into the layers of shale and sandstone, some propped up by trapezes of thick, roughly-hewn beams, others reinforced by a thick stone lining. All around, the seams eaten up by the exploitation had been replaced by infilling: in other words artificial pillars had been made from stones, dug from neighbouring quarries, and were now supporting the ground, that is the double level of Tertiary and Quarternary strata, which had in the past rested on top of the coal seam itself. Darkness now filled these tunnels, long ago lit up either by the miner's lamp or electric light, the use of which had been introduced in the pits during the last years. But the sombre tunnels no longer resounded with the creaking of wagons rolling on the rails, nor the sound of the air doors slamming shut, nor the shouts of the putters, nor the neighing of horses and mules, nor the blows of the workers' pick-axes, nor the blasts of dynamite that exploded the rock.

'Do you want to rest a minute, Mr Starr?' asked the young man.

'No, my boy,' replied the engineer, 'for I am eager to reach old Simon's cottage.'

'Follow me then, Mr Starr. I will guide you, although I am sure that you remember your way perfectly through this dark maze of tunnels.'

'Yes, indeed! I still have the whole plan of the old pit in my head.'

Harry, followed by the engineer and lifting his lamp better to light him, entered a high tunnel which resembled the nave of a cathedral. Their feet were still treading on the wooden sleepers that supported the rails during the period of exploitation.

But they had barely made fifty steps when an enormous stone came crashing to the feet of James Starr.

'Be careful, Mr Starr!' cried Harry, grabbing the engineer's arm.

'A stone, Harry! Ah! These old vaults are not solid enough anymore, and no doubt...'

'Mr Starr,' replied Harry Ford, 'it seems to me that the stone was thrown... and thrown by the hand of a man!'

'Thrown!' cried James Starr. 'What do you mean, my boy?'

'Nothing, nothing... Mr Starr', replied Harry evasively, whose suddenly serious look could have pierced the thick walls of rock. 'Let's continue on our way. Take my arm, please, and have no fear of making a false step.'

'Here I am, Harry!'

And the two of them advanced, with Harry continually looking behind them, projecting the light of the lamp into the depths of the tunnel.

Jack Ryan

'Will we soon be there?' asked the engineer.

'In ten minutes at the most.'

'Good.'

'But,' murmured Harry, 'that is no less strange. That's the first time anything like that has happened to me. The stone had to fall just at the moment when we were passing...'

'Harry, it was just a coincidence.'

'A coincidence...' replied the young man, shaking his head. 'Yes... a coincidence...'

Harry stopped. He listened.

'What is it, Harry?' asked the engineer.

'I thought I heard footsteps above us,' replied the young miner, who listened more attentively.

Then he said, 'No, I must have been mistaken. Lean well on my arm, Mr Starr. Use me like a stick...'

'A solid stick, Harry,' replied James Starr. 'There is none better than a brave boy such as you!'

The two continued to walk silently along the gloomy nave.

Harry, obviously preoccupied, frequently turned round, trying to catch either a far off noise, or some distant light.

But behind and before them there was nothing but silence and shadows.

CHAPTER FIVE

The Ford Family

TEN MINUTES LATER, James Starr and Harry finally came out of the main tunnel.

The young miner and his companion had arrived at the bottom of a clearing – if that word can be used to describe a vast and dark hollow. This hollow was not, however, completely devoid of daylight. Some rays reached it through the mouth of an abandoned shaft that had been sunk into the higher floors. It was through this conduit that Dochart Pit's air current was established. Because of its lesser density, the hot air of the interior was drawn out through the Yarrow Shaft.

So a little air and light penetrated the thick shale vault to the clearing.

It was here that Simon Ford had been living with his family for the last ten years. A subterranean dwelling, dug out of the solid shale, in the very place where the powerful machines for working the mechanical haulage of Dochart Pit had once operated.

Such was the abode – which he called a 'cottage' – where the old overman resided. Some savings accumulated during his long working life would have allowed Simon Ford to live in full sunlight, surrounded by trees, in any village in the kingdom; but he and his family had preferred not to leave the mine where they were happy, sharing the same ideas and tastes. Yes! They liked that cottage, buried fifteen hundred feet beneath the Scottish soil. Among other advantages, they had nothing to fear from the 'stentmasters', the agents responsible for the poll tax, who never ventured down there to pester the residents!

Simon Ford, the former overman of Dochart Pit, still bore his sixty-five years lightly. Tall, robust, well-built, he was regarded

Simon Ford

as one of the most outstanding 'sawneys'[6] of a district that has provided many a handsome man to the Highland regiments.

Simon Ford was descended from an old mining family, and his genealogy went back to the period when carbon-bearing seams were first exploited in Scotland.

Without researching archaeologically into whether the Greeks and Romans used coal, whether the Chinese used coal mines well before the Christian era, and without discussing whether the combustible mineral really owes its French name *houille* to Houillos the blacksmith, who lived in Belgium in the twelfth century, it is known that the coalfields of Great Britain were the first to be regularly exploited. Already by the eleventh century, William the Conqueror shared the produce of the Newcastle coalfields amongst his companions in war. In the thirteenth century, Henry III granted an exploitation licence for 'sea-coal'. Finally, around the end of the same century, mention is made of the coal seams of Scotland and Wales.

It was around this time that Simon Ford's ancestors entered the depths of the Caledonian soil, to live there ever after from father to son. They were simple workmen. They toiled like slaves in the extraction of the precious fuel. It is even thought that the coal miners, just like the workers in the salt-works at this period, were in fact real slaves. Indeed, in the eighteenth century this view was so well established in Britain that twenty thousand miners in Newcastle revolted to regain their freedom – something they believed they did not have.

Whatever he was, Simon Ford was proud of belonging to this great family of Scottish miners. He had worked with his hands, at the very place where his ancestors had handled the pick, the crowbar, the double-pointed pick and the pickaxe. At thirty, he was overman of Dochart Pit, the most important of the Aberfoyle mines. He loved his profession passionately. For long

---

[6] A 'sawney' is the term for a Scotsman, just as John Bull is the Englishman and Paddy the Irishman.

years, he carried out his duties with zeal. His only sorrow was to see the layer grow thinner and to predict the approaching hour when the seam would be exhausted.

It was then that he devoted himself to the search for new seams in all the Aberfoyle pits, which were interconnected beneath the ground. He had the good fortune to discover several during the last period of exploitation. His miner's instinct served him well and the engineer James Starr strongly appreciated it. It was said that he divined the seams in the bowels of the mine like a hydroscope divines underground streams.

But the moment came, as has been said, when the mine was completely devoid of fuel. The surveys no longer yielded any result. It was clear that the coal seams were completely exhausted. Exploitation ceased. The miners had to go.

Could it be believed? The majority despaired. All who recognise that Man, deep down, loves labour, will not be surprised. Simon Ford was unquestionably the most affected. He was, *par excellence*, the kind of miner whose existence is inextricably linked to that of his mine. Since his birth, he had never lived anywhere else, and when the operations were abandoned, he wanted to remain there. So there he stayed. His son Harry was responsible for delivering provisions to the underground dwelling; but as for himself, he had not mounted to the surface ten times in ten years.

'Go up there! Why?' he would say, and would not leave his black domain.

Besides, in this perfectly healthy environment, always moderate in temperature, the old overman experienced neither the heat of summer, nor the cold of winter. His family were well. What more could he want?

Deep down, he was profoundly saddened. He missed the liveliness, the movement, the life of the past, in the pit once so busily worked. However, he was sustained by a fixed belief.

'No! Never! The mine is not exhausted!' he would repeat.

And anyone who expressed his doubts in front of Simon

Ford that one day old Aberfoyle would be brought back from the dead would have regretted it! So he had never given up hope of discovering some new seams which would restore the mine to its former glory. If necessary, he would willingly have taken up his miner's pick and vigorously attacked the rock with his still sturdy old arms. He would go through the dark tunnels, sometimes alone, sometimes with his son, observing, searching, to return to the cottage each day tired, but not despairing.

Simon Ford's worthy companion was Madge, who was tall and strong, and his 'good wife' as the Scottish expression goes. Madge had not wanted to leave Dochart Pit any more than her husband. In this respect she shared all his hopes and regrets. She encouraged him, she pushed him on, she spoke to him with a kind of earnestness that warmed the old overman's heart.

'Aberfoyle is just asleep, Simon,' she would say. 'You are right. It's just resting, it isn't dead!'

Madge too knew how to do without the external world and to concentrate on the happiness of life for three in the dark cottage.

It was here that James Starr had now arrived.

The engineer was indeed expected. Simon Ford, standing in front of his door, saw Harry's lamp announce the arrival of his former 'viewer' and advanced towards him.

'Welcome, Mr James!' he cried in a voice that echoed under the shale vault. Welcome to the cottage of your old overman! The Ford family house is no less welcoming for being buried fifteen hundred feet under the earth!'

'How are you, my good Simon?' asked James Starr, shaking the hand extended by his host.

'Very well, Mr Starr. And how could it be otherwise here, sheltered from the intemperance of the atmosphere? Your ladies, who go to take the air at Newhaven or Portobello[7] during the summer, would do better to spend a few days in the Aberfoyle coalmines! They would have no risk of catching a nasty cold

---

[7] Seaside resort near Edinburgh.

here, as they do in the damp streets of the old capital.'

'It is not I who would say otherwise, Simon,' replied James Starr, happy to find the overman unchanged. 'I wonder, really, why I do not swap my house in the Canongate for a cottage neighbouring yours!'

'At your service, Mr Starr. I know one of your old miners who would be perfectly delighted to have nothing but a shared wall between him and yourself.'

'And Madge?' asked the engineer.

'The good wife is even better than I am, if that's possible!' replied Simon Ford, 'and it is a joy for her to see you at her table. I think that she will excel herself in receiving you.'

'Let's find out, Simon, let's find out!' said the engineer, who could not be left indifferent by the announcement of a good lunch, after the long walk.

'Are you hungry, Mr Starr?'

'Positively famished. The journey has worked up my appetite. I came through dreadful weather!'

'Ah! It's raining up there!' replied Simon Ford with a marked air of pity.

'Yes, Simon, and the Forth was as rough as the sea today!'

'Ah well, Mr James, here it never rains. But I don't need to tell you about advantages that you know as well as I! Well here you are arrived at the cottage. That's the main thing, and I repeat, you are very welcome!'

Simon Ford, followed by Harry, showed James Starr into the dwelling. He found himself in the middle of a huge room, lit by several lamps, one of which was suspended from the coloured joists of the ceiling.

The table, covered by a brightly coloured tablecloth, lacked only the diners, for whom four old leather-covered chairs were placed.

'Good morning, Madge,' said the engineer.

'Good morning, Mr James,' replied the good Scotswoman, who rose to receive her guest.

'I'm glad to see you again, Madge.'

'And so you should be, Mr James, for it is pleasant to meet up with people you have always treated well.'

'The soup is waiting, dear,' said Simon Ford, 'and you mustn't make it wait, any more than Mr James. He has a miner's appetite, and he will see that our boy doesn't let us go without anything in the cottage! By the way, Harry,' added the old overman, turning towards his son, 'Jack Ryan came to see you.'

'I know, father. We met him in the Yarrow Shaft.'

'He's a good lad, and a jolly companion,' said Simon Ford. 'But he seems to like it up there! He doesn't have real miner's blood in his veins. Let's sit down, Mr James, and eat heartily, for we might not be able to have supper until much later.'

'Just a moment, Simon,' said James Starr. 'Do you want me to eat with a healthy appetite?'

'That will give us the greatest honour, Mr James,' replied Simon Ford.

'Well, for that I must not have any preoccupation. For I have two questions to put to you.'

'Go ahead, Mr James.'

'Your letter spoke of some information that would interest me?'

'It is very interesting, indeed.'

'For you?'

'For you and for me, Mr James. But I want to give it to you after the meal, and in the place itself. Otherwise, you wouldn't believe me.'

'Simon,' resumed the engineer, 'look directly at me... in the eyes. Some interesting information...? Good! ... I shall not press you further,' he added, as if he had read the response he was hoping for in the old overman's expression.

'And the second question?' he asked.

'Do you know, Simon, who could have written this?' replied the engineer, presenting the anonymous letter that he had received.

Madge

Simon Ford took the letter and read it very carefully.

Then, showing it to his son, he said:

'Do you recognise this writing?'

'No, father.'

'And this letter had the Aberfoyle postmark on it?' Simon Ford asked the engineer.

'Yes, like your one,' replied James Starr.

'What do you make of that, Harry?' said Simon Ford, whose brow darkened for an instant.

'I think, father,' replied Harry, 'that someone had some interest in preventing James Starr from coming to the appointment that you had given him.'

'But who?' cried the old miner. 'Who could have penetrated so far into my mind's secrets?'

And a pensive Simon Ford fell into a trance, soon awakened by Madge's voice.

'Let's sit down, Mr Starr,' she said, 'the soup will get cold. Let's not think any more about that letter for the time being!'

And, on the invitation of the old woman, they each took their place at the table – James Starr did Madge the honour of sitting opposite her, with father and son opposite one another.

It was a good Scottish meal. First, they ate 'hotchpotch', a soup of meat swimming in an excellent stock. According to old Simon, his wife had no rival in the art of making hotchpotch.

It was the same, moreover, for the 'cock-a-leeky' – a sort of chicken ragoût made with leeks – which earned nothing but praise.

That lot was washed down with an excellent ale, drawn from the best breweries of Edinburgh.

But the main dish was a 'haggis', the national meat and oatmeal pudding. This notable dish, which inspired one of the poet Robert Burns' best odes, had the fate reserved for the finer things of this world: it passed like a dream.

Madge received the sincere compliments of her guest.

The meal ended with a dessert of cheese and fine oatcakes,

accompanied by a small glass of 'usquebaugh', an excellent grain whisky, which was twenty-five years old – exactly the age of Harry.

The meal lasted an hour. James Starr and Simon Ford not only ate heartily, but they had also talked heartily – principally about the past of the old Aberfoyle mine.

As for Harry, he had stayed rather quiet. He had twice left the table and even the house. It was clear that he was somewhat uneasy since the incident with the stone, and he wanted to check the vicinity of the cottage. The anonymous letter had done nothing to reassure him.

It was during one of his absences that the engineer said to Simon Ford and Madge:

'That's a brave lad that you have there, my friends!'

'Yes, Mr James, a good and devoted son,' replied the old overman eagerly.

'Is he happy with you, in the cottage?'

'He wouldn't want to leave us.'

'You would consider marrying him, though?'

'Marry him!' cried Simon Ford. 'And to whom? A girl from up there, who would like parties and dancing, who would prefer her clan to our coalmine! Harry wouldn't want it!'

'Simon,' rebuked Madge gently, 'for all that you wouldn't forbid our Harry from ever taking a wife...'

'I'm not forbidding anything,' replied the old miner, 'but there is no hurry! Who knows but we won't find him one...'

Harry came back at that moment, and Simon Ford kept quiet.

When Madge rose from the table, the others followed and came to sit a moment at the cottage door.

'Ah well, Simon,' said the engineer, 'I am listening!'

'Mr James,' replied Simon Ford, 'It's not your ears I need, but your legs. Are you well rested?'

'Well rested, and well refreshed, Simon. I am ready to accompany you wherever you please.'

'Harry,' said Simon Ford, turning towards his son, 'light our safety lamps.'

'You are taking safety lamps!' cried James Starr, somewhat surprised as firedamp explosions were no longer a threat in a pit completely devoid of carbon.

'Yes, Mr James, as a precaution!'

'Are you not also going to suggest that I dress myself as a miner, my good Simon?'

'Not yet, Mr James! Not yet!' replied the old overman, whose eyes shone peculiarly from their deep sockets.

Harry, who had gone back inside the cottage, came out again almost immediately carrying three safety lamps.

Harry gave one of these lamps to the engineer, another to his father, and kept the third hanging from his left hand, while his right hand was armed with a long stick.

'Let's go!' said Simon Ford, who took up a solid pickaxe, left at the cottage door.

'Lead on!' replied the engineer. 'Goodbye, Madge!'

'God help you!' replied the Scotswoman.

'A good supper, mind, my good wife,' cried Simon Ford. 'We'll be hungry when we get back, and we'll do you proud!'

CHAPTER SIX

Some Inexplicable Phenomena

WE ARE FAMILIAR with the superstitious beliefs of the Highlands and Lowlands of Scotland. In certain clans, the tenants of the laird, gathered for an evening, love to retell stories taken from the repertoire of far northern mythology. Rational education, however widely and liberally spread through the country, has not yet been able to destroy the belief in these legends, which seem inherent to the very soil of old Caledonia. It is still a land of spirits and ghosts, imps and fairies. The malevolent spirit that only goes away in exchange for money still makes its appearance there, as does the Seer of the Highlanders who through a gift of second sight foretells approaching deaths; May Moullach, who appears in the form of a young girl with hairy arms and warns families of the misfortunes threatening them; the banshee, who heralds disastrous events; brownies, who are trusted with the protection of the household; Urisks, who frequent most specifically the wild gorges of Loch Katrine; and many others.

It goes without saying that the population of the Scottish mines must add its contingent of legends and fables to this mythological repertoire. If the mountains of the Highlands are peopled by chimerical creatures, good and bad, all the more reason that the dark coalmines must be haunted down to their greatest depths. Who makes the seam tremble during stormy nights? Who marks out the still unexploited seam? Who lights the firedamp and presides over the terrible explosions, if not some spirit of the mine? That was, at least, the commonly-held opinion of the superstitious Scots. In truth, most of the miners readily believed in the fantastical where purely physically phenomena were concerned, and you would be wasting your time

'Goodbye, Madge!' said the engineer.

in trying to disabuse them of this. Nowhere was credulity developed more freely than at the bottom of these abysses.

Now, the Aberfoyle mines, precisely because they were exploited in the land of legends, must have lent themselves rather easily to supernatural incidents.

Legends abounded there. It must be said, moreover, that certain, until then unexplained, phenomena could not but further feed public credulity.

Leading the ranks of the superstitious of Dochart Pit was none other than Harry's friend Jack Ryan. No one was a greater believer in the supernatural than he. He transformed all these fantastical stories into songs, which earned him great success during those winter evenings.

But Jack Ryan was not the only one to display this superstition. His friends maintained, with as much vigour, that the Aberfolye pits were haunted, that certain elusive creatures frequently appeared there, just as happened in the Highlands. To hear them talk, you would think it extraordinary if this were not the case. Was there, indeed, an environment better disposed to the frolics of spirits, bogles, will o' the wisps and other actors of fantastical dramas than a deep and dark coalmine? The set was ready-made – why would the supernatural characters not come to play their part?

So reasoned Jack Ryan and his friends of the Aberfoyle mines. We have said that the various pits communicated by long underground tunnels, arranged between the seams. Under Stirlingshire there was therefore an enormous mass, crisscrossed with tunnels, hollowed with caves, drilled by shafts – a sort of hypogeum, an underground labyrinth, like a vast ant-hill.

The miners of the various pits therefore met each other often, either when they were going to work at coal-faces, or when they were returning from them. This provided a constant facility for exchanging theories and circulating stories originating in the mine from one pit to another. The tales were transmitted by word of mouth in this way with great rapidity and inevitable exaggeration.

However, two men, with more education and of a more rational temperament than the rest, had always resisted this impulse. They would not concede the least intervention of bogles, spirits or fairies.

They were Simon Ford and his son. They proved it by continuing to live in the dark crypt, after the abandonment of Dochart Pit. Perhaps good Madge had some inclination to the supernatural, like every Highland Scotswoman. But she was reduced to recounting these stories of apparitions to herself – which she did conscientiously moreover, so as not to forget the old traditions.

Even if Simon and Harry Ford had been as gullible as their friends, they would never have abandoned the mine, not to spirits nor to fairies. The hope of discovering a new seam would have made them brave any fantastical cohort of bogles. But they were not credulous – their faith ran in one direction: they could not admit that the carboniferous deposit of Aberfoyle had been totally exhausted. You could say, with some reason, that Simon Ford and his son had in this matter 'the faith of the coalman', a faith in God that nothing could shake.

That is why for ten years, without missing one single day, father and son, obstinate and unshakeable in their convictions, took up their picks, their sticks and their lamps. They went together, looking, testing the rock with clean blows, listening for a favourable sound.

As long as the soundings had not penetrated down as far as the granite of the Primary layer, Simon and Harry Ford were agreed that the search, fruitless today, could be fruitful tomorrow, and that it should be continued. They had spent their entire lives trying to restore the Aberfoyle mines to their past prosperity. If the father should die before the hour of success, the son would carry on the task alone.

At the same time, these two passionate guardians of the mine inspected it with its conservation in mind.

They made sure of the solidity of the cutting infills and the vaults. They checked whether there was a risk of tunnel collapses, and whether it was urgent to condemn some part of the pit. They examined the signs of infiltration of streams from above, re-routed them, and canalised them to divert them to some well. In short, they willingly became the protectors and conservationists of this unproductive place, from which had come so much wealth, now gone up in smoke!

It was during some of these excursions that Harry, in particular, happened to be struck by certain phenomena, the causes of which he searched in vain.

Thus, several times, when he followed some narrow cross-tunnel, he seemed to hear noises resembling the violent blows of a pickaxe hitting an infill wall.

Harry, who could no more be scared by the natural than by the supernatural, had hurried to discover the cause of this mysterious work.

The tunnel was deserted. The young miner's lamp, shining on the wall, did not reveal any trace of recent crowbar or pick blows. So Harry wondered if it hadn't been the trick of some acoustic illusion, some strange or weird echo.

Other times, on suddenly projecting a bright light towards a suspicious crevice, he thought he saw a shadow passing. He dashed forward... Nothing, despite the fact that there was no exit that would have allowed a man to give him the slip.

Twice this last month, while visiting the west part of the pit, Harry distinctly heard far-off detonations, as if a miner had exploded a stick of dynamite.

On the most recent occasion, after painstaking research he discovered that a pillar had been blown apart by a mine blast.

In the light of his lamp, Harry carefully examined the wall struck by the mine. It had not been made by simply infilling with stones, but from a section of shale, which had penetrated to this depth in the level of the coal deposit. Was the purpose of the mine blast to provoke the discovery of a new seam? Had

In the light of his lamp, Harry carefully examined the wall.

someone wanted to collapse this part of the coalmine? That was what Harry wondered, and when he made this fact known to his father, neither he nor the old overman were able to resolve the question satisfactorily.

'It is strange,' Harry would often repeat. 'The presence of an unknown being in the mine seems impossible, and yet it cannot be doubted! Does someone other than us want to discover whether there isn't still some exploitable seam? Or rather is he trying to destroy what remains of the Aberfoyle mines? But to what end? I'll find out, if it costs me my life!'

A fortnight before this day when Harry Ford was guiding the engineer through the maze of Dochart Pit, he found himself on the brink of successfully concluding his searches.

He was roaming through the extremity of the south-west of the mine, a powerful lamp in hand.

Suddenly, it seemed to him that a faint light had just been extinguished some few hundred feet before him, at the bottom of a narrow chimney that cut obliquely into the rock mass. He hurried towards the suspicious light...

A fruitless search. As Harry refused to accept supernatural explanations for physical things, he concluded that an unknown person must be lurking in the pit. But, whatever he did, searching with the utmost care, scrutinising the slightest crevices in the tunnel, he gained nothing for his trouble and was unable to arrive at any certain conclusion.

So Harry left it to chance to uncover this mystery. Here and there, he still saw glimmers of light appear, which fluttered about from one point to another like St Elmo's Fire; but they lasted just a flash and he had to give up trying to discover their cause.

If Jack Ryan and the other superstitious folk of the colliery had seen these fantastical flames, they would have certainly blamed them on the supernatural!

But that did not even cross Harry's mind. Nor old Simon's. And when the two of them talked about these phenomena, obviously due to a purely physical cause, the old overman would say, 'My boy, let us wait! Some day all that will be explained!'

In any case, it should be noted that never, until then, had either Harry or his father been exposed to an act of violence.

If the stone, fallen at James Starr's feet that very day, had been thrown by an ill-intentioned hand, it was the first criminal act of this type.

James Starr, when asked, was of the opinion that this stone had come loose from the roof of the tunnel. But Harry did not accept such a straightforward explanation. The stone, in his view, had not fallen: it had been thrown. Unless it had rebounded, it would never have followed that trajectory if not cast by an external force.

Harry therefore saw in it a direct attempt against him and his father, or even against the engineer. From what we know, perhaps he had good reason for thinking so.

CHAPTER SEVEN

Simon Ford's Experiment

THE OLD WOODEN CLOCK in the sitting-room was striking midday as James Starr and his two companions left the cottage.

The light that penetrated through the ventilation shaft vaguely lit the clearing. Harry's lamp was therefore redundant, but would serve before long for the old overman was going to take the engineer towards the extremity of Dochart Pit.

After following the principal tunnel for a distance of two miles, the three explorers – for we shall see that it was an exploration – reached the mouth of a narrow tunnel. It was like a nave, with the vaulting supported by timberwork carpeted in a whitish moss. It followed more or less the route of the Forth fifteen hundred feet above.

In case James Starr had forgotten the labyrinth that was Dochart Pit, Simon Ford reminded him of the general plan, comparing it to the geographical layout at ground level.

James Starr and Simon Ford were therefore talking as they walked.

Harry was in front, lighting the way. He was trying to discover some suspicious shadow by suddenly projecting bright beams of light into dark crevices.

'Are we going much further, Simon, old man?' asked the engineer.

'Another half-mile, Mr James. In the past we would have made this journey by truck, on the mechanical haulage trams. But those days are long gone!'

'So are we heading to the end of the last seam?' asked James Starr.

'Yes! I see that you still know the mine well.'

'Ah, Simon,' replied the engineer, 'it would be difficult to go further, if I am not mistaken?'

'Indeed, Mr James. It was there that our two-pointed picks tore out the last lump of coal from the seam. I remember it as if I were still there! I dealt the final blow, and it resounded in my heart more violently than in the rock! There was nothing but sandstone and shale left around us, and when the wagon rolled towards the production shaft, I followed it, with a heavy heart, as one follows a funeral procession. It seemed to me that the soul of the mine was going with it!'

The seriousness with which the old overman pronounced these words affected the engineer, for he was not far himself from sharing such sentiments. They are the feelings of the sailor who abandons his wrecked ship, of the lord who sees the house of his ancestors demolished.

James Starr had already shaken Simon Ford's hand. But, in turn, the latter had just taken the engineer's hand, and squeezing it tightly said:

'That day, we were all mistaken. No! The old coalmine wasn't dead! What the miners had just abandoned was not a corpse, and I would dare to swear, Mr James, that its heart is still beating!'

'Speak then, Simon! Have you discovered a new seam?' cried the engineer, who could not contain himself. 'I knew it! Your letter could not have meant anything else! Some information to be given to me, and to be given in Dochart Pit! And what discovery other than that of a coal-bearing layer could have interested me?'

'Mr James,' replied Simon Ford, 'I didn't want to inform anyone other than yourself...'

'And you did well to do so, Simon! But tell me how, by what surveys have you convinced yourself...?'

'Listen, Mr James,' replied Simon Ford. 'It isn't a seam that I have found...'

'What is it then?'

'Only the material proof that this seam exists.'

'And this proof?'

'Could you accept that firedamp could be released from the innards of the earth without coal there to produce it?'

'No, certainly not!' replied the engineer. 'No coal, no firedamp! There is no effect without a cause...!'

'Like there is no smoke without fire!'

'And you have observed, anew, the presence of carburetted hydrogen?'

'An old miner doesn't let himself be taken unawares,' replied Simon Ford. 'I recognised our old enemy, the firedamp.'

'But what if it was another gas?' said James Starr. 'Firedamp is colourless and practically odourless. It only truly betrays its presence by an explosion!'

'Mr James,' replied Simon Ford, 'if you would allow me to tell you what I have done... and how I did it... in my way, for-giving me if it takes some time?'

James Starr knew the old overman, and knew that it was best to let him go on.

'Mr James,' resumed Simon Ford, 'there has not been one day these last ten years that Harry and I have not dreamt of restoring the mine to its former prosperity – not one day! If some seam still existed, we were determined to find it. What method should we use? Surveys? They were impossible for us, but we had our miner's instinct, and instinct often leads more directly to a goal than reason. At least that's my belief...'

'Which I would not argue with,' replied the engineer.

'Now, here's what Harry had observed once or twice during his excursions to the west of the coalmine. Some flames, which suddenly went out, appeared several times across the shale or the infill of the furthermost tunnels. What was causing these fires to flare up? I could not and I still cannot say. But still, these flames obviously could only be the result of the presence of firedamp, and for me, firedamp means coal.'

'Did these flames not produce any explosion?' asked the engineer, energetically.

'Yes they did – small, partial explosions,' replied Simon Ford, 'and ones such as I provoked myself, when I wanted to test for the presence of firedamp. Do you remember the way in which we tried to anticipate explosions in the mines in the past, before our great genius Humphrey Davy invented his safety lamp?'

'Yes,' replied James Starr. Do you mean the 'penitent'? But I have never seen one at work.'

'Indeed, Mr James, despite being fifty-five you are too young to have seen that. But being ten years older than you, I saw the last penitent working in the mine. We called him that because he wore a large monk's robe. The correct term was the 'fireman'. At that time we didn't have any way of destroying the harmful gas other than burning it off through small explosions before its lack of density caused it to gather in dangerously large quantities high in the tunnels. That's why the penitent, with a mask on his face, his head hooded in a thick balaclava, and his whole body tightly squeezed into his monk's frock would crawl along the ground. He would breathe at the low layers, where the air was pure, and would proceed with a flaming torch lifted in his right arm above his head. When the firedamp was diffused in the air so as to form an explosive mixture, a non-fatal explosion would occur, and by repeating this operation regularly, we succeeded in avoiding disasters. Sometimes, caught in a firedamp explosion, the penitent died for his trouble. Another would replace him. It was like this until the Davy lamp was adopted in all the coalmines. But I knew the procedure, and it was by using it that I identified the presence of firedamp and, consequently, of a new carbon-bearing deposit in Dochart Pit.'

All that the old overman had recounted about the penitent was thoroughly accurate. In the past the air in mine tunnels was purified in this manner.

Firedamp, otherwise known as carburetted hydrogen or marsh gas, is colourless, nearly odourless, has limited lighting

The penitent, with a mask on his face... would crawl along the ground.

power, and is entirely unsafe to breathe. A miner could no more survive in a place filled with this harmful gas than he could survive in a gasometre-full of gas for lighting. Moreover, just as with this latter gas, which is methane, firedamp forms an explosive mixture when air mixes with it in a proportion of eight, perhaps even five, percent. Something or other ignites this mixture and there is an explosion, nearly always causing a dreadful disaster.

The Davy lamp avoids this danger by isolating the lamp's flame in a tube of metallic gauze so that it burns the gas inside the tube without ever allowing the flame to spread outside. This safety lamp has been perfected in a score of ways. If it breaks, the flame goes out. If, despite all its structural defences, the miner wants to open it, it goes out again. Why then do these explosions occur? It is because nothing can prevent the carelessness of a worker who wants to light his pipe, or the impact of a tool that can produce a spark.

Not all coalmines are infected by firedamp. In those where it does not occur, the use of the ordinary lamp is allowed. Thiers Pit in the Anzin mines of Northern France is one such case. But a bitumous coal seam contains a significant quantity of volatile material and firedamp can escape in great abundance. The safety lamp alone is devised to prevent explosions that are all the more terrible since the miners not directly killed by the firedamp explosion risk being instantaneously asphyxiated in the tunnels filled with noxious gas formed after the combustion, in other words, by carbonic acid.

While they walked, Simon Ford informed the engineer of what he had done to achieve his purpose, how he was sure that the firedamp was being released at the very bottom of the pit's furthest tunnel, in the western part, and how he had provoked some partial explosions – or rather small flames – where the shale layers surfaced, which left him in no doubt as to the nature of the gas, which leaked in small but continuous quantities.

An hour after leaving the cottage, James Starr and his two

companions had covered a distance of four miles. The engineer, spurred on by desire and hope, made this journey without ever thinking about its length. He was reflecting on all that the old miner was telling him. He mentally weighed the arguments that the latter had given him to support his theory. He too believed that this continual emission of carburetted hydrogen pointed unmistakeably to the existence of a new coal-bearing seam. If it had been only a sort of gas-filled pocket, like he had sometimes come across between layers, it would have quickly emptied, and the phenomenon would have ceased to occur. But that was far from being the case. According to Simon Ford, the hydrogen escaped endlessly, and from that could be concluded the existence of an important seam. Consequently, the riches of Dochart Pit could not be entirely exhausted. However, were they talking about a layer with a yield of little consequence, or of a coalfield covering a large surface of coal-bearing land? There, indeed, lay the great question.

Harry, who was ahead of his father and the engineer, came to a stop.

'Here we are!' cried the old miner. 'Finally, by the grace of God, Mr James, you are here, and we will find out...'

The normally steady voice of the old overman was trembling slightly.

'My good Simon,' said the engineer, 'calm yourself. I am as moved as you are, but we must not waste time!'

In this place, the furthest tunnel of the pit flared out into a sort of dark cavern. No shaft had been sunk into this part of the rock, and the tunnel, deeply dug into the bowls of the earth, had no direct communication with the surface of Stirlingshire.

James Starr, keenly interested, examined the place where he found himself with a careful eye.

On the end wall of this cavern you could still see the marks of the last blows of the pickaxe, and even some holes from cartridges that had split the rock towards the end of the exploitation. This shale material was extremely hard and it had not been

The Davy Lamp

necessary to fill in the foundations of this cul-de-sac, at the end of which the work had had to stop. It was here, between the shale and the sandstone of the Tertiary rocks, that the carboniferous seam had died out. Here, at this very spot, the last lump of fuel from Dochart Pit had been extracted.

'Here, Mr James,' said Simon Ford, lifting his pick, 'we will attack the fault[8] here, for behind this wall, at a greater or lesser depth, must certainly lie the new seam that I know exists.'

'And it is at the surface of these rocks,' asked James Starr, 'that you have observed the presence of firedamp?'

'The very same, Mr James,' replied Simon Ford, 'and I was able to light it just by approaching my lamp to where the layers surface. Harry has done it too.'

'At what height?' asked James Starr.

'Ten feet from the ground,' replied Harry.

James Starr was sitting on a rock. One might have said that, after inhaling the air of the cavern, he looked at the two miners as if he was ready to doubt their, nonetheless very positive, words.

For the fact is that carburetted hydrogen is not completely odourless, and the engineer was above all surprised that his sense of smell, which was very acute, did not reveal the presence of the explosive gas to him. In any case, if this gas was mixed with the ambient air, it was only in a very slight dose. So, with no explosion to fear, they could open the safety lamp without danger to conduct the experiment, just as the old miner had done before.

It was not that there might be too much gas mixed in the air that was worrying James Starr at this moment, but rather that there might not be enough – even none at all.

'Are they mistaken?' he murmured. 'No! These are men who know their stuff! And yet...'

---

[8] The fault is the part of the rock mass which lacks the seam and is normally made up of sand stone or shale.

He waited therefore rather anxiously for the phenomenon reported by Simon Ford to occur in his presence. But, at that moment, it seemed that what he had just observed, that is to say the absence of the characteristic smell of firedamp, had also been noticed by Harry, for he said, in an altered voice:

'Father, the gas no longer seems to be leaking through the cracks between the layers!'

'No longer there!' cried the old miner.

And Simon Ford, after tightly sealing his lips, sighed loudly through his nose several times.

Then, suddenly, and with a brusque movement he said:

'Give me your lamp, Harry!'

Simon Ford took the lamp with a feverishly shaking hand. He unscrewed the metallic gauze covering which encircled the wick, and the flame burned freely in the air.

Much as it was awaited, no explosion occurred; but, what was more serious, there was not even the light sparking that indicates the presence of a feeble amount of firedamp.

Simon Ford took the stick that Harry was holding and, fixing the lamp at one end, he lifted it to the upper layers of the air, where because of its characteristic lightness the gas would have accumulated, in whatever minimal quantity there might be.

The flame of the lamp, straight and white, detected no trace of carburetted hydrogen.

'At the wall!' said the engineer.

'Yes!' replied Simon Ford, holding the lamp to the part of the wall through which just the day before he and his son had observed the flow of gas.

The old miner's arm was trembling as he tried to pass the lamp to the height of the cracks in the layer of shale.

'Take over, Harry,' he said.

Harry took the stick and presented the lamp successively to various points of the rock where the layers seemed to split...but he was shaking his head, for the light crackling, particular to escaping firedamp, did not reach his ear.

No flame was produced. It was therefore clear that not one molecule of gas was passing through the rock.

'Nothing!' cried Simon Ford, who extended his fist, more in anger than in disappointment.

A cry escaped from Harry's mouth.

'What is it?' asked James Starr eagerly.

'Someone has filled the cracks in the shale!'

'Are you sure?' cried the old miner.

'Look, father!'

Harry was not mistaken. The blockage of the cracks was clearly visible in the light of the lamp. A recently made lime filling left a long whitish trace on the wall, badly hidden under a layer of coal dust.

'Him!' cried Harry. 'It could only be him!'

'Him?' repeated James Starr.

'Yes!' replied the young man, 'this mysterious being who haunts our territory, for whom I've been on the lookout a hundred times, without being able to catch him, the author, it is now certain, of the letter which tried to prevent you from coming to the appointment which my father gave you, Mr Starr, and he, lastly, who threw that stone at us in the tunnel of the Yarrow Shaft! Ah! There is no possible doubt! A man's hand is behind all this!'

Harry had spoken with such energy that his conviction passed instantly and completely into the engineer's mind. As for the old overman, he did not need convincing. Moreover, they found themselves confronted with an undeniable fact: the blocking of the cracks through which the gas had freely passed the day before.

'Take your pickaxe, Harry,' cried Simon Ford. 'Climb on my shoulders, my boy! I am still sturdy enough to carry you!'

Harry had understood. His father leant against the rockface. Harry climbed onto his shoulders so that his pickaxe could reach the quite visible trace of the filling. Then, with increasingly forceful blows, he broke open the part of the shale rock that had been filled.

Immediately a light fizzing was produced, like Champagne when it leaves a bottle – a sound that in British coalmines goes by the onomatopoeic name 'puff'.

Harry then grabbed the lamp and approached the crack...

A light explosion was produced, and a little red flame, slightly bluish at the edges, flickered on the rockface, like an apparition of St Elmo's fire.

Harry immediately jumped to the ground, and the old overman, unable to contain his joy, seized the engineer's hands crying:

'Hurrah! Hurrah! Hurrah! Mr James! The firedamp is burning! So the seam is there!'

He broke open the part of the shale rock...

CHAPTER EIGHT

A Blast of Dynamite

THE OLD OVERMAN'S experiment had succeeded. Carburetted hydrogen, it is known, develops only in coal deposits. Therefore, the existence of a seam of the precious fuel could no longer be doubted. What was its size and quality? We shall find out later.

Such were the conclusions that the engineer deduced from the phenomenon that he had just observed. They accorded completely with those of Simon Ford.

'Yes,' said James Starr to himself, 'behind this wall lies a coal-bearing layer which our surveys were unable to reach. That is unfortunate, because all the equipment of the mine, abandoned ten years ago, now needs to be reinstalled. Never mind! We have rediscovered the seam that we believed exhausted, and this time, we shall exploit it right up to the last!'

'Well, Mr James,' asked Simon Ford, 'what do you think of our discovery? Was I wrong to bother you? Are you regretting this last visit to Dochart Pit?'

'No, no, my old friend!' replied James Starr. 'We have not wasted our time, but we will be wasting it now if we do not return to the cottage immediately. Tomorrow, we shall come back here. We shall blast this wall with dynamite. We shall bring to light the surface of the new seam, and after a series of surveys, if the layer seems to be significant, I will create a New Aberfoyle Company, to the extreme satisfaction of the old shareholders! The first tubs of coal should be extracted from the new seam before three months are up.'

'Well said, Mr James!' cried Simon Ford. 'The old mine will be rejuvenated, like a widow who remarries! The life of the old days will begin again with the blows of axes and picks, the blasts of mines, the rolling of wagons, the neighing of horses, the rumbling of machines! I shall see all that again, I shall!'

'I hope, Mr James, that you won't find me too old to resume my duties as overman?'

'No, my good Simon, certainly not! You have stayed younger than me, my old friend!'

'And may St Mungo protect us! You shall be our viewer again! May the work last many long years, and may Heaven grant me the consolation to die before seeing it end!'

The old miner's joy overflowed. James Starr shared it completely, but he let Simon Ford enthuse for them both.

Only Harry remained pensive. The succession of strange, inexplicable circumstances surrounding discovery of the new seam kept coming back to him. It worried him for the future.

One hour later, James Starr and his two companions were back at the cottage.

The engineer supped with a hearty appetite, approving with a gesture all the plans which the old overman was developing, and had it not been that he was impatient for the coming day, he would have slept better than ever in the absolute calm of the cottage.

The next day, after a substantial meal, James Starr, Simon Ford, Harry, and Madge as well, took the route already travelled the previous day. They all went as veritable miners. They carried various tools and cartridges of dynamite, destined to blow up the end wall. As well as a powerful lantern, Harry took a large safety lamp that could burn for twelve hours. It was more than would be needed for the return journey, including the stops necessary for the exploration – if an exploration became possible.

'To work!' cried Simon, when he and his companions had reached the end of the tunnel.

And he seized a heavy crowbar in his hand, brandishing it energetically.

'One moment,' said James Starr. 'Let us look to see if anything has changed and if firedamp is still diffusing through the layers in the wall.

'You're right, Mr Starr,' replied Harry. 'What was blocked up yesterday could well be so again today!'

Madge, seated on a rock, had her attention fixed on the cave and the wall that was to be blown open.

It was observed that things were as they had left them. The cracks in the layers had not undergone any alteration. The carburetted hydrogen was leaking through, but quite feebly. That was no doubt because it had found a free passage through which to spread since the previous day. In any case, this emission was of such little significance that it could not combine with the interior air to form an explosive mixture. James Starr and his companions were therefore able to proceed in complete security. Moreover, this air gradually purified itself in reaching the high levels of Dochart Pit, and the firedamp, lost in this atmosphere, would be unable produce any explosion.

'To work, then!' repeated Simon Ford.

And, under his vigorously handled crowbar, it was not long before rock was flying in fragments.

This fault was composed principally of pudding stone, located between the sandstone and the shale, as is very often encountered at the outcropping of carbon-bearing seams.

James Starr gathered up the pieces that the tool had broken off, and he examined them carefully, hoping to find in them some indication of coal.

This initial work took about an hour. It resulted in quite a deep hollow in the end wall.

James Starr then chose the place for the shot holes to be dug, work that was quickly accomplished by Harry with a hammer and foil.[9]

Dynamite cartridges were put into these holes. As soon as the long, tarred wick of the safety fuse, which terminated at a percussion cap, had been positioned there it was lit at ground level.

---

[9] A special type of mining chisel.

James Starr and his companions moved back.

'Ah! Mr James,' said Simon Ford, gripped by a palpable emotion that he made no effort to conceal, 'never, no never, has my old heart beaten so quickly! I already want to attack the seam!'

'Patience, Simon,' replied the engineer. 'You are not expecting to find a completely open tunnel behind this wall?'

'Excuse me, Mr James,' replied the old overman. 'I have every possible expectation! If Harry and I had good luck in the way we discovered this deposit, why shouldn't this luck continue right up to the end?'

The dynamite exploded. A deafening rumble spread across the network of underground tunnels.

James Starr, Madge, Harry and Simon Ford immediately returned to the cavern wall.

'Mr James! Mr James!' cried the old overman. 'Look! The door is broken open...'

Simon Ford's comparison was justified by the appearance of a hole, whose depth could not be guessed.

Harry made to rush forward through the opening...

The engineer, extremely surprised, as it happened, to find this cavity, held back the young miner.

'Give the air inside time to circulate,' he said.

'Yes! Watch out for the foulness!'[10] cried Simon Ford.

They spent an anxious quarter of an hour waiting. The lantern, hung on the end of a stick, was then introduced into the hole and it continued to burn with an unfailing brightness.

'Go on then, Harry,' said James Starr, 'we'll follow you.'

The opening produced by the dynamite was more than enough for a man to pass through.

Harry, lamp in hand, went in without hesitation and disappeared into the shadows.

---

[10] Name given to harmful fumes in coalmines.

74

One minute passed – though it seemed much longer. Harry did not reappear, he did not call out. Approaching the orifice, James Starr did not even see the glow of his lamp, which should have lit up this dark cavity.

Had the ground suddenly disappeared under Harry's feet? Had the young miner fallen into some crevice? Could his voice no longer reach his companions?

The old overman, not wanting to listen, made to enter the opening in his turn, when a glow appeared, dim at first, then gradually stronger, and Harry made himself heard:

'Come, Mr Starr! Come, father! The road to New Aberfoyle is open.'

Harry, lamp in hand, went in without hesitation...

CHAPTER NINE

New Aberfoyle

IF, BY SOME superhuman power, engineers had been able to lift in one block a thousand feet thick the whole section of the Earth's crust that bears the lochs, rivers, inlets, banks and braes of Stirlingshire, Dumbartonshire and Renfrewshire, they would have found under this enormous lid a vast hollow, the like of which exists only one other example in the world – the famous Mammoth Cave in Kentucky.

The cave consisted of several hundred alveoli cavities, of all shapes and sizes. It could be called a hive, with its numerous levels of capriciously placed cells, but a hive built on a huge scale, and which rather than bees, would have adequately lodged all the ichthyosaurs, megatheria, and pterodactyls of the geological era.

A labyrinth of tunnels – some higher than the highest cathedral vaults, others like narrow and twisting naves, some following a horizontal line, others climbing and descending diagonally in all directions – connected the caves and allowed free communication between them.

The pillars that supported the vaults, curved in all styles, the thick walls, solidly seated between the tunnels, and the naves themselves in this floor of Secondary rocks, were made of sandstone and shale rocks. But between these unusable layers, and forcefully squeezed by them, ran admirable veins of coal, as if the black blood of this strange coalmine circulated through their complex system. These deposits developed over a surface of forty miles from north to south, and they even extended under the North Channel. The basin's importance could only be evaluated after surveys, but it must have exceeded the coal-bearing layers of Cardiff, in Wales, and the coalfields of Newcastle in the county of Northumberland.

It should be added that the exploitation of this coalmine would be singularly facilitated because, through the strange disposition of the secondary rocks, through an inexplicable dissolution of mineral materials during the geological era when this mass solidified, Nature had already created multiple tunnels and passageways in New Aberfoyle.

Yes, Nature alone! It could have been believed at first that some exploitation abandoned centuries ago had been discovered. It was nothing of the sort. Such riches are not abandoned. The human termites had never eaten into this part of subterranean Scotland, and it was Nature who had made things so. But, I repeat, no hypogeum of the Egyptian period, nor catacomb of the Roman period, could have compared with it – nothing except the famous Mammoth Cave which, over a length of more than twenty miles, counts two hundred and twenty-six avenues, eleven lakes, seven rivers, eight waterfalls, thirty-two unfathomable shafts and fifty-seven domes, some of which are suspended from a height of more than four hundred and fifty feet.

New Aberfoyle, like these caverns, was the work not of man, but of the Creator.

Such was this new domain, of incomparable richness, the discovery of which was entirely due to the old overman. Ten years of residence in the old mine, a rare persistence in his searches, an absolute faith, supported by an exceptional miner's instinct – it had taken all these qualities together to succeed where so many others would have failed. Why had the surveys of the last years of the exploitation, conducted under James Starr's direction, stopped precisely at this limit, on the very frontier of the new mine? It was down to chance, whose part in explorations of this kind is great.

Whatever the reason, there beneath Scotland was a sort of subterranean county, which in order to be habitable needed only the rays of the sun, or failing that, the brightness of a special star.

Water was located in certain depressions, forming vast ponds, even lochs larger than Loch Katrine, situated precisely above. No doubt these lochs lacked the movement of waters, currents and backwashes. They did not reflect the silhouette of some old gothic castle. Neither birches, nor oaks hung over their banks; no mountains laid great shadows on their surface; steamboats did not cut across them; no light reflected in their waters; the sun did not soak its bright rays; and the moon never rose on their horizon. And yet, these deep lochs, whose surfaces were not rippled by any breeze, would not be without charm in the light of some electric star, and, connected by a chain of canals, they complemented well the geography of this strange domain.

However unsuitable for all production of vegetation, this was a place that could, nonetheless, accommodate an entire underground population. And who knows, when their seams are exhausted, these temperate places at the bottom of the Aberfoyle coalmines, as well as those in Newcastle, Alloa and Cardiff – who knows that they might not some day provide a refuge for the working classes of the United Kingdom?

CHAPTER TEN

Coming and Going

ON HARRY'S CALL, James Starr, Madge and Simon Ford entered the narrow mouth that connected Dochart Pit with the new mine.

The found themselves at the beginning of a rather large tunnel. One would have thought that it had been dug out by Man, that the pick and pickaxe had emptied it for the exploitation of a new seam. The explorers must have wondered if they had not by some chance been transported into some old coalmine, which even the oldest miners of the county had never known.

No! It was the geological beds that had 'spared' this tunnel, at the period when the Secondary rocks were compressed. Perhaps some torrent had run there in the past, when the overlying water came to mix with the muddy vegetation: but now, it was as dry as if it had been drilled some thousand feet lower, in the underlying granitic rocks. At the same time, the air freely circulated there – which indicated that certain natural 'vents' put it in communication with the outside atmosphere.

This observation, made by the engineer, was accurate, and one sensed that the ventilation would operate easily in the new mine. As for the firedamp which yesterday was seeping through the shale of the wall, it seemed that it had been contained just in a simple 'pocket', now empty, and it was clear that there was not the least trace if it in the tunnel's atmosphere. However, as a precaution, Harry had brought only the safety lamp, which would give him light for twelve hours.

James Starr and his companions were feeling utter joy. All their desires had been completely satisfied. There was nothing but coal all around them. A particular kind of emotion kept them silent. Even Simon Ford was holding himself back. His joy overflowed, not in long sentences, but through little interjections.

It was perhaps imprudent of them to go so deeply into the crypt. Pah! They rarely thought about the return. The tunnel was passable, almost straight. No crevasse barred the way, no propulsion of air spread harmful exhalations. Therefore there was no reason to stop, and James Starr, Madge, Harry and Simon Ford proceeded thus for an hour, without having any indication of the exact orientation of this unknown tunnel.

And no doubt they would have carried on further still, had they not reached the very extremity of this wide path that they had followed since entering the mine.

The tunnel came to an end in an enormous cavern, the height and depth of which could not be guessed. At what altitude did the vault of this cave curve? What was the distance to the opposite wall? The shadows filling it prevented these details being known. But, in the glow of the lamp, the explorers could tell that its dome spanned a vast stretch of dormant water – a lagoon or loch – whose picturesque banks, broken up by high rocks, were lost in the darkness.

'Halt!' cried Simon Ford, stopping abruptly. 'One step further, and we might roll into some abyss!'

'Let us rest then, my friends,' replied the engineer. 'We should think about going back to the cottage as well.'

'Our lamp can light us for another ten hours yet, Mr Starr,' said Harry.

'Just so, but let us stop anyway,' resumed James Starr. 'I swear that my legs need it! And you, Madge, do you not feel tired after such a long walk?'

'Not really, Mr James,' replied the sturdy Scotswoman. 'We're used to exploring the old Aberfoyle mines for whole days at a time.'

'Pah!' added Simon Ford, 'Madge would do this walk ten times over if necessary! But I insist, Mr James: did my informa-

A lagoon or loch – whose picturesque banks...

tion merit being given to you? Dare to say no, Mr James, dare to say no!'

'Ah yes, old friend, it has been a long time since I have felt such joy!' replied the engineer. 'The little that we have explored of this marvellous coalmine seems to show that its expanse is very considerable, at least in length.'

'In breadth and in depth as well, Mr James!' returned Simon Ford.

'We shall find that out later.'

'I tell you now! Depend on my old miner's instinct. It has never let me down!'

'I want to believe you, Simon,' replied the engineer, smiling. 'But still, from what I can judge from this short exploration, we have the elements of an exploitation that will last centuries!'

'Centuries!' cried Simon Ford. 'I can well believe it, Mr James! A thousand years and more will pass before the last lump of coal will be extracted from our new mine!'

'May God hear you!' replied James Starr. 'As for the quality of the coal which shows on the surface of these walls...'

'Superb, Mr James, superb!' replied Simon Ford. 'See for yourself!'

And saying this he broke off a fragment of black rock with a blow of his pick.

'Look! Look!' he repeated, bringing his lamp to it. 'The surfaces of this piece of coal are glistening! We have here top quality bituminous coal! And how it breaks into good-sized nuggets,[11] almost without dust! Oh, Mr James, twenty years ago this seam would have made tough competition for Swansea or Cardiff! Well the stokers will argue over it again, and it won't sell for any less outside for being cheap to extract from the mine!'

'Indeed,' said Madge, who had taken the fragment of coal and was examining it knowledgeably. 'Now that's good quality

---

[11] Name that miner's give to medium-sized coal.

coal. Take it, Simon, take it to the cottage! I want this first piece of coal to burn in our stove!'

'Well said, my dear,' replied the old overman, 'and you will see that I am not mistaken.'

'Mr Starr,' asked Harry now, 'have you any idea of the probable orientation of this long tunnel that we have followed since our entering the new mine?'

'No, my boy,' replied the engineer. 'With a compass, I would be able to establish its general direction. But without a compass, I am here like a sailor out at sea, surrounded by mist, who cannot read his position for the absence of the sun.'

'No doubt, Mr James,' rejoined Simon Ford, 'But, please, don't compare our situation to that of a sailor, who always and everywhere has the abyss below his feet! We are on solid ground here, and we have no fear of sinking!'

'I will spare you that suffering, Simon,' replied James Starr. 'It is far from my thoughts to deprecate the new coalmine of Aberfoyle by an inaccurate comparison! I only wanted to say one thing: that we do not know where we are.'

'We are beneath Stirlingshire, Mr James,' replied Simon Ford, 'and that, I confirm as if...'

'Listen!' said Harry, interrupting the old overman.

They all joined the young miner in lending an ear. His very practised auditory nerve had detected a dull noise, like a faraway murmur. James Starr, Simon and Madge were not long in hearing it themselves. A sort of rumbling was coming from the upper layers of the rock mass, and, feeble as it was, successive *crescendos* and *decrescendos* could be distinctly made out.

All four remained for some minutes, ears strained, without saying a word.

Then suddenly Simon Ford cried:

'By St Mungo! Do wagons already run on the rails of New Aberfoyle?'

'Father,' replied Harry, 'it seems to me that it is the sound that the waters make rolling on a shore.'

'Yet we aren't under the sea!' cried the old overman.

'No,' replied the engineer, 'but it would not be impossible that we are under the very bed of Loch Katrine.'

'The roof of the vault must be very thin in this part for the sound of the waters to be perceptible?'

'Very thin, indeed,' replied James Starr, 'and that is what makes this cavern so vast.'

'You must be right, Mr Starr,' said Harry.

'Moreover, the weather is so bad outside,' replied James Starr, 'that the waters of the loch must be raised up like the Firth of Forth.'

'Oh, what does it matter, after all?' replied Simon Ford. 'The coal-bearing layer won't be any the worse for having developed under a loch! It wouldn't be the first time that man has gone under the very bed of the ocean to look for coal! When the time comes when we will have to exploit the coal under the sea floor and depths of the North Channel, where will be the harm?'

'Well said, Simon,' cried the engineer, who could not suppress a smile while watching the enthusiastic overman. 'Let's extend our trenches under the waters of the sea! Let's riddle the bed of the Atlantic with holes! Let's go and join our brothers in the United States by pickaxe blows beneath the ocean! Let's dig down to the centre of the earth, if we must, to cut out the last lump of coal!'

'Are you joking, Mr James?' asked Simon Ford, nonetheless rather pleased.

'Me, joking, Simon old chap? No! But you are so enthusiastic, that you are carrying me away to the realm of the impossible! Come on, let's get back to reality, which is already wonderful enough. Let's leave our picks here, which we will recover another day, and head back to the cottage!'

There was nothing else to do for the moment. Later, the engineer, accompanied by a team of miners and equipped with the necessary lamps and tools, would resume the exploration of New Aberfoyle. But it was imperative to return to Dochart Pit.

Besides, the road was easy. The tunnel ran almost straight across the mass of rock up to the mouth opened by the dynamite. There was, therefore, no fear of losing the way.

But, just when James Starr was heading towards the tunnel, Simon Ford stopped.

'Mr James,' he said, 'do you see this huge cavern, this underground lake that it covers, this shore that the waters come to bathe at our feet? Well, I want to move my home here, I will build myself a new cottage here, and if some brave companions want to follow my example, within a year we'll have one town more in the rock of our old Scotland!'

James Starr, approving Simon Ford's projects with a smile, shook his hand, and all three, preceded by Madge, disappeared into the tunnel to rejoin Dochart Pit.

The first mile was without incident. Harry was walking in front, holding the lamp above his head. He carefully followed the main tunnel, never venturing off into the narrow tunnels that radiated left and right. It appeared, therefore, as if the return should be accomplished as easily as the outgoing journey, when an unfortunate complication arose, which turned the explorers' situation very grave.

For just when Harry lifted his lamp, a strong gust of air was produced, as if caused by the beating of invisible wings. The lamp, caught at an angle, escaped Harry's hands, fell on to the rocky ground of the tunnel and smashed.

James Starr and his companions were suddenly plunged into absolute darkness. Their lamp, with its oil spilt, could no longer be used.

'Good Lord, Harry,' cried Simon Ford, 'do you want us to break our necks going back to the cottage?'

Harry did not reply. He was reflecting. Did he again detect the hand of a mysterious being in this last accident? Was there an enemy in these depths whose inexplicable antagonism could one day cause serious difficulties? Did someone have an interest in defending the new coal deposit against all attempts at

A strong gust of air was produced...

exploitation? In truth, that was absurd, but the facts spoke for themselves, and they were accumulating so as to change simple presumptions into certainties.

Meanwhile, the explorers' situation was rather serious. They would have to follow the tunnel that led to Dochart Pit for about five miles, surrounded by deep shadows. Then, they would have another hour's walk before reaching the cottage.

'Let's carry on,' said Simon Ford. 'We have no time to lose. We'll grope our way along, like the blind. It isn't possible to get lost. The tunnels that open onto our path are really just as if in molehills, and by following the main tunnel, we'll inevitably reach the mouth that let us through. Then, it's the old coalmine. We know it, and it won't be the first time than Harry and I have found ourselves there in the dark. Besides, we'll find the lamps that we have left there. So, let's go! Harry, take the lead. Mr James, you follow him. Madge, you'll come after, and I'll bring up the rear. Above all, don't let us split up, and we should keep on each other's heels, if not elbows!'

They had only to follow the instructions of the old overman. As he said, by groping their way they could hardly take the wrong path. They had simply to replace their eyes with their hands, and trust in that instinct which to Simon Ford and his son had become second nature.

So James Starr and his companions walked in the order indicated. They did not speak, but that was not for lack of thinking. It was becoming clear that they had an adversary. But who was it, and how could they defend themselves against these attacks, so mysteriously prepared? These rather worrying ideas flooded their brains. However, this was not the moment to get discouraged.

Harry, arms stretched out, advanced with an assured step. He went successively from one tunnel wall to the other. A cavity or a lateral opening would present itself, and he recognised with his hand where not to go, whether the crevice was shallow, whether the opening was too narrow, and thus kept on the right path.

In the middle of a darkness to which their eyes could not get accustomed, because it was so absolute, this difficult return took about two hours. By calculating the time passed, taking account of the fact that the walk had necessarily not been fast, James Starr estimated that he and his companions must be very close to the end.

Indeed, at almost the same time, Harry stopped.

'Have we finally reached at the end of the tunnel?' asked Simon Ford.

'Yes,' replied the young miner.

'Well then, you should find the mouth that established communication between New Aberfoyle and Dochart Pit.'

'No,' replied Harry, whose tense hands recognised only the full surface of a wall.

The old overman took some steps forward, and came to feel the shale rock himself.

He let out a cry.

Either the explorers had gone astray during their return, or the narrow mouth cut in the wall by the dynamite had recently been refilled!

Whichever it was, James Starr and his companions were imprisoned in New Aberfoyle.

He let out a cry.

CHAPTER ELEVEN

The Fire-Maidens

EIGHT DAYS AFTER these events, James Starr's friends were very worried. The engineer had disappeared without any motive being attributable to this disappearance. They had learned, by questioning his maid, that he had embarked at Granton Pier, and they knew from the captain of the *Prince of Wales* steamboat that he had disembarked at Stirling. But since then, not a trace of James Starr. Simon Ford's letter had recommended secrecy, and he had not said a word about his departure for the Aberfoyle coalmines.

Therefore, in Edinburgh, the only matter in question was the engineer's inexplicable absence. Sir W Elphiston, the president of the Royal Institution, communicated to his colleagues the letter that James Starr had addressed to him, excusing himself for being unable to attend the Society's next meeting. Two or three other people produced similar letters. But, if these documents proved that James Starr had left Edinburgh – which was already known – there was nothing to indicate what had become of him. Now, on the part of such a man, this unusual absence necessarily caused first surprise, then concern, as it was prolonged.

None of the engineer's friends could have imagined that he had gone to the Aberfoyle coalmines. It was known that he did not want to return to his former workplace. He had not set foot there since the day that the last tub had been raised to ground level. Nevertheless, because the steamboat had dropped him off at the landing-stage at Stirling, some enquiries were made there. These came to nothing. Nobody recalled having seen the engineer in the area. Only Jack Ryan, who had met him in Harry's company on one of the landings of the Yarrow Shaft, would have been able to satisfy the public curiosity. But as we know, the cheerful lad was working at Melrose Farm, forty miles away in south-west Renfrewshire, and he hardly guessed that there was such anxiety about the disappearance of James Starr. So, eight days after his visit to the cottage, Jack Ryan would have continued to sing his heart out during the Irvine clan festival – had not he too had a very worrying concern, about which more later.

James Starr was a man too considerable and too considered, not only in the city, but in the whole of Scotland, for anything concerning him to pass unnoticed. The Lord Provost, the highest Edinburgh magistrate, the baillies, the advisers, most of whom were friends of the engineer, began the most active enquiries. Officers were sent into the countryside, but to no avail.

The situation therefore demanded that an announcement on the engineer James Starr's disappearance, giving his description and indicating the date on which he had left Edinburgh, be placed in Scotland's main newspapers, and there was nothing more to do but wait. Time did not pass without the greatest anxiety. The British educated class was not far from contemplating the permanent loss of one of its most distinguished members.

At the same time that the person of James Starr was causing worry, the person of Harry was the subject of preoccupations no less acute. Except that instead of being a public concern, the old overman's son troubled only the good humour of his friend Jack Ryan.

We remember that when they met in the Yarrow Shaft, Jack Ryan had invited Harry to come, eight days later, to the Irvine clan festival. Harry had accepted and formally promised to come to this ceremony. Jack Ryan knew, from experience, that his friend was a man of his word. With him, a promise made was a promise kept.

Now, at the Irvine festival nothing was missing, not songs, nor dances, nor festivities of every kind, nothing – except Harry Ford.

Jack Ryan had begun by holding this against him, because the absence of his friend had deflated his good humour. He even had a lapse of memory in the middle of one of his songs, and for the first time he was at a loss during a jig, which normally brought him well-deserved applause.

It must be said here that the announcement relating to James Starr, published in the newspapers, had not yet fallen under Jack Ryan's eyes. This brave lad therefore was concerned solely about Harry's absence, telling himself that only a serious situation could have prevented Harry from keeping his promise. Consequently, the day after the Irvine festival, Jack Ryan was planning on taking the Glasgow railway to go to Dochart Pit, and would have done so – had he not been delayed by an accident that could have cost him his life.

Here is what happened during the night of the 12th of December. In fact, the nature of the event provided confirmation to all those believers in the supernatural – and at Melrose Farm they were many.

Irvine, a little maritime town in Renfrewshire, with about seven thousand inhabitants, is built in a sharp bend in the Scottish coast, almost at the mouth of the Firth of Clyde. Its port, quite well sheltered from the sea winds, is lit up by a large beacon, which indicates the landing-points so that no careful sailor can make a mistake. Therefore, shipwrecks are rare on this part of the coastline, and whether they wish to take the Firth of Clyde to get to Glasgow, or to dock in Irvine Bay, the coasters or packet-ships are able to manoeuvre without danger, even on dark nights.

When a town is furnished with an historic past, however meagre, when its castle once belonged to one Robert Stuart, it is not without some ruins.

Now in Scotland, all ruins are haunted by ghosts. At least that is the popular belief in the Highlands and Lowlands.

The most ancient ruins, and also the most infamous of this part of the coastline, were precisely those of the castle of Robert

Stuart, which bore the name of Dundonald Castle.

At this period, Dundonald Castle, refuge of all the wandering imps of the land, was destined to the most total abandon. People seldom went to visit it on the high rock that it occupied above the sea, two miles from the town. Perhaps some strangers still had the notion of investigating these old historic remains, but in that case they went there alone. The inhabitants of Irvine would not drive them there at any price. For there were stories going round about certain 'fire-maidens' that haunted the old castle.

The most superstitious claimed to have seen these fantastical creatures with their own eyes. Naturally, Jack Ryan was one of them.

The fact of the matter is that, from time to time, long flames would appear, now on a half-crumbled section of wall, now at the top of the tower which dominated the array of ruins of Dundonald Castle.

Did these flames have a human shape, as was claimed? Did they merit the name 'fire-maidens' which the Scots of the coast had given them? Obviously, there was nothing there other than an optical illusion to which some real form was imputed, and science would have provided some physical explanation.

Whatever it was, throughout the land the fire-maidens had a well-established reputation of frequenting the ruins of the old castle and of sometimes carrying out strange dances there, especially on dark nights. Jack Ryan, bold fellow as he was, would never dare accompany them with the sounds of his bagpipes.

'Old Nick is enough for them!' he would say, 'And there's no need for me to complete their infernal orchestra!'

It would be right to assume that these bizarre apparitions constituted the obligatory text for the evening story-telling. Jack Ryan had a whole repertoire of legends about the fire-maidens, and never found himself at a loss where tales on this subject were concerned!

So, during this last evening, awash with ale, brandy and whisky, at the climax of the Irvine clan festival, Jack Ryan did not fail to reprise his favourite theme, to the great pleasure, and perhaps great terror, of his audience.

The evening was held in a huge barn at Melrose Farm, on the edge of the coast. A hearty coke fire was burning in a large cast iron tripod brazier in the middle of the gathering.

Outside the weather was terrible. Thick mists rolled on the waves, which a strong south-westerly wind brought from the open sea. It was a very black night, not a single clearing in the clouds, and earth, sky and water were indistinguishable in the deep shadows – this would make landings at Irvine Bay difficult, were some vessel venturing through these gales that were battering the coast.

The little port of Irvine was not much used – at least by ships above a certain tonnage. The commercial sailing or steam ships come towards the land a little further north when they want to take the Firth of Clyde.

This particular evening, however, some fisherman, out late on the shore, perceived, with some surprise, a ship heading towards the coast. If daylight had suddenly arrived, it would have been not just with surprise, but with terror, that this ship would have been seen, racing with a tail wind and with all the sails that it could bear. The entrance to the Firth missed, there was no other refuge between the formidable rocks of the coast. If this reckless ship persisted in coming in closer, how would it manage to get out again?

The evening was going to finish on one last story from Jack Ryan. His listeners, transported into a world of phantoms, were ready to believe anything – should the need arise.

Suddenly, cries resounded from outside.

Jack Ryan immediately stopped his story, and everyone hurried out of the barn.

It was in the depths of night. Long gusts of wind and rain were lashing the surface of the shore.

Two or three fishermen, pressed up near a rock, so as better to resist the force of the wind, were shouting violently.

Jack Ryan and his companions ran to them.

These cries were not addressed to the inhabitants of the farm, but to a crew who, without knowing it, were rushing towards their death.

Indeed, a dark mass was vaguely apparent at several cable lengths. It was a ship, clearly recognisable by its navigation lights, for it was carrying a white light at its foresail mast, a green light at the starboard side, and a red light at the port side. It was therefore being viewed from the front, and it was clear that it was heading towards the coast at full speed.

'A ship in distress?' cried Jack Ryan.

'Yes,' replied one of the fishermen, 'and now it wants to tack, which it can no longer do!'

'Signals, signals!' cried one of the Scotsmen.

'Which ones?' replied the fisherman. 'In this squall, we couldn't keep a torch alight!'

And, during these rapid exchanges, new shouts were hurled. But how could they be heard in the midst of this storm? The ship's crew would have no chance of escaping shipwreck.

'Why manoeuvre in that way?' cried a sailor.

'Does it want to run aground, then?' replied another.

'So the captain is unfamiliar with the lights of Irvine?' asked Jack Ryan.

'You would think so,' replied one of the fisherman, 'unless he has been tricked by some...'

The fisherman had not finished his sentence when Jack Ryan gave an awesome cry. Did the crew hear it? In any case, it was too late for the ship to get out of the line of breakers, which gleamed white in the shadows.

But Jack Ryan was not, as might have been believed, trying to get one last warning across to the ship in distress. Jack Ryan had his back to the sea. His companions, too, were looking at a point half a mile into the shore.

It was Dundonald Castle. A long flame was twisting under the gusts at the top of the old tower.

A dark mass was vaguely apparent... It was a ship...

'Fire-maidens!' cried all these superstitious Scots with great terror.

Frankly, it required a good dose of imagination to find a human appearance in this flame. Agitated like a luminous flag under the wind, it sometimes seemed to disappear from the top of the tower, as if it had been on the point of going out, and, a moment later, its bluish tip returned again.

'The fire-maiden! The fire-maiden!' cried the terrified fishermen and peasants.

So everything was explained. It was clear that the ship, disoriented in the mists, had made a false course, and had taken this flame, lit at the summit of Dundonald Castle, for the Irvine beacon. It thought that it was at the entrance to the Firth, ten miles further north, and it was sailing towards steep land that provided no shelter!

What could be done to save it, if there was still time? Perhaps they should climb up to the ruins and try to put out the fire, so that it would no longer be possible to confuse it with the Irvine port signal!

Without doubt, this was the appropriate action to take, without delay; but which of these Scots would have the thought, and, after the thought, the audacity to brave the fire-maiden? Jack Ryan, perhaps, for he was courageous, and his superstition, strong as it was, could not have stopped him from a selfless action.

It was too late. A horrible cracking resounded from the midst of the crashing elements.

The ship's rear had just scraped the bottom. Its navigation lights went out. The whitish line of the surf seemed to be momentarily broken. The ship was colliding with it, lying down on its side and smashing up between the reefs.

And, at the same instant, by a coincidence that could only be due to chance, the long flame disappeared, as if uprooted by a violent gust. The sea, sky and shore were immediately plunged back into the darkest shadows.

'The fire-maiden!' cried Jack Ryan one last time, when this – for him and his companions – supernatural apparition suddenly vanished.

But then, the courage that these superstitious Scots would not have had against a chimerical danger, they rediscovered faced with real danger, now that it concerned saving their fellow men. The unleashed elements would not stop them. Using ropes thrown into the waves they leaped to the aid of the wreck – as heroic as they had been credulous.

Fortunately, they succeeded, but not without some men – and bold Jack Ryan was one of them – being seriously bruised on the rocks; but the ship's captain and the eight men of the crew were deposited, safe and sound, on the shore.

The ship was the Norwegian brig, the *Motala*, loaded with wood from the north, heading for Glasgow.

It was all too real. The captain, tricked by the fire lit on the tower of Dundonald Castle, had come aground in open shore, instead of entering the Firth of Clyde.

And now there remained nothing of the *Motala* but a few pieces of wreckage, which the surf finished off, smashing the debris against the coastal rocks.

The furious waves had dashed him brutally against the reefs.

CHAPTER TWELVE

Jack Ryan's Exploits

JACK RYAN AND three of his companions, injured like himself, were transported to one of the rooms of Melrose Farm, where they were immediately attended to.

Jack Ryan had suffered the worst, for just when he had leaped into the sea with the rope around his back, the furious waves had dashed him brutally against the reefs. Indeed he was lucky that it was not his corpse that was brought ashore.

The brave lad was therefore confined to his bed for some days – which infuriated him. However, when he was allowed to sing as much as he wanted to, he bore his pain with patience, and Melrose Farm resounded at all hours with the joyous bursts of his voice. But from this adventure Jack Ryan drew only a stronger feeling of fear of these brownies and other imps that took pleasure in plaguing the poor world, and it was them he held responsible for the *Motala* disaster. He would not be open to suggestions that the fire-maidens did not exist, and that this flame, rising so suddenly between the ruins, was a purely physical phenomenon. No reasoning could convince him. His companions were still more obstinate than him in their beliefs. According to them, one of the fire-maidens had maliciously attracted the *Motala* to the coast. As for wanting to punish them, you might as well fine a storm! The magistrates could instigate all the prosecutions that they liked. You cannot imprison a flame, you cannot chain up an intangible being. And, if it needs to be said, the enquiries that were later made, appeared to support – at least superficially – this superstitious way of explaining things.

For the magistrate charged with directing an enquiry into the loss of the *Motala* came to question the various witnesses of the disaster. All were agreed on one point, that the shipwreck was due to the supernatural apparition of the fire-maiden in the ruins of Dundonald Castle.

One can well understand that the justice could not go along with such reasoning. There could be no doubt that some purely physical phenomenon occurred in the ruins. But was it an accident or malevolence? That was the question that the magistrate ought to have tried to establish.

This word 'malevolence' should not surprise us. One does not have to go far back into Roman Gallic history to find justification. Many a pillager of wrecks on the Brittany coast practiced this trade of attracting ships onto the rocks in order to share the spoils. A clump of resinous trees, lit during the night, would guide a ship into channels from which there was no way out. A torch, attached to the horns of a bull moving about at the animal's whim, would fool a crew into following the wrong course. The result of these manoeuvres was inevitably a shipwreck, from which the pillagers profited. It had taken the intervention of the judiciary and exemplary punishments to put an end to these barbaric practices. Now, could it not be that in this instance a criminal hand was at work in reviving the forgotten traditions of the wreckers?

That is what the police authorities thought, whatever Jack Ryan and his companions said. When the latter heard talk of an investigation, they divided into two camps: those who were content to shrug their shoulders; and those more fearful souls, who were in no doubt that provoking supernatural beings like this would bring new disasters.

Nevertheless, the enquiry was carried out very scrupulously. A police team went to Dundonald Castle and proceeded with the most thorough investigations.

The magistrate wanted first to discover whether the ground had conserved any footprints that could be attributed to feet other than those of imps. But it was impossible to find the faintest impression, new or old. Yet the earth, still damp from the previous day's rain, would have conserved the slightest trace.

'Brownie's footsteps!' cried Jack Ryan, when he learned of the failure of these first investigations. 'You might as well look for the traces of a will o' the wisp in the water of a bog!'

This first part of the investigation therefore produced no result. It was unlikely that the second part would yield anything more.

For its purpose was to establish how fire could have been lit at the top of the old tower, what elements had been used to light the flame, and finally, what traces had this combustion left.

On the first point there was nothing, neither the remains of matches, nor scraps of paper, which could have served to light a fire.

On the second point the lack of evidence was no less absolute. They found neither dried grass, nor pieces of wood, with which this fire, which burned so intensely, would have had to have been continually stoked during the night.

As for the third point, no more light could be shed on that. The total absence of ashes or of any residue of any fuel whatsoever, made it impossible even to identify the area in which the fire must have been made. There was no blackened area, neither on the ground nor on the rock. Should it then be concluded that the fire had been held in the hand of some criminal? This was very improbable since, according to the witnesses, the flame had displayed gigantic proportions, so that despite the fog the *Motala*'s crew had been able to see it from several miles at sea.

'Good!' cried Jack Ryan, 'The fire-maiden can do without matches! She only has to blow for the air to flare up around her, and her hearth leaves no ashes!'

The result of all this was that all the magistrates got for their trouble was a new legend to add to so many others – a legend that the memory of the *Motala* disaster would perpetrate and affirm still more incontestably the apparition of the fire-maidens.

Meanwhile, such an active lad as Jack Ryan, of such a vigorous constitution, could not stay in bed for long. A few sprains and dislocations were not going to keep him lying on his back longer than necessary. He did not have time to be ill. When time is short, one is rarely ill in the healthy regions of the Lowlands.

So Jack Ryan promptly recovered. As soon as he was on his feet, before resuming his work at Melrose Farm, he wanted to carry out a particular project. It involved going to visit his friend Harry to find out why he had missed the Irvine clan festival. For a man like Harry, who never made a promise without keeping it, this absence was inexplicable. It was incredible, moreover, that the former overman's son had not heard about the *Motala* disaster reported in great detail by the newspapers. Surely he would know the part that Jack Ryan had played in the rescue and what had happened to him, and it was uncharacteristic indifference on Harry's part not to come straight to the farm to shake his friend Jack Ryan by the hand.

If, then, Harry had not come, it was because he could not come. Jack Ryan would rather deny the existence of fire-maidens than believe Harry indifferent to his well-being.

So, two days after the disaster, Jack Ryan cheerfully left the farm as a hearty lad who felt none of his injuries. He made the echoes of the cliff resound with a joyful refrain bellowed out with full lungs, and took himself to the railway station, which went to Stirling and Callander via Glasgow.

While he was waiting in the station there, his eyes were immediately captured by a poster, plastered all over the walls, containing the following announcement:

'On the 4th December, the engineer James Starr, of Edinburgh, embarked at Granton Pier on the *Prince of Wales*. He disembarked the same day at Stirling. Since this time, we are without news of him.

'Please address any information regarding him to the President of the Royal Institution, Edinburgh.'

Jack Ryan stopped in front of one of these posters and read it twice over, not without showing signs of extreme astonishment.

'Mr Starr!' he cried. 'But on the 4th December exactly I met him with Harry on the ladders of the Yarrow Shaft. That was ten days ago! And he hasn't reappeared since! Does this explain why my friend didn't come to the Irvine festival?'

And, without taking the time to inform the President of the Royal Institution by letter of what he knew about James Starr, the brave lad jumped on the train, with the firm intention of going directly to the Yarrow Shaft. Once there, he would descend to the bottom of Dochart Pit if necessary, to find Harry, and with him the engineer James Starr.

Three hours later, he left the train at Callander Station, and headed quickly for the Yarrow Shaft.

'They have not reappeared,' he said to himself. 'Why? Is some obstacle preventing them from doing so? Is some important work still keeping them down at the bottom of the mine? I shall find out!'

And Jack Ryan, hurrying along, arrived at the Yarrow Shaft in less than an hour.

From the outside, nothing had changed. The same silence in the pit's surroundings. Not a living soul in this desert.

Jack Ryan entered under the ruined lean-to which covered the mouth of the shaft. He thrust his eyes into this abyss... He saw nothing... He listened... He heard nothing.

'And my lamp!' he cried. 'Should it not be in its place?'

The lamp, which Jack Ryan used during his visits to the pit, was normally placed in a corner near the landing of the upper ladder.

The lamp had vanished.

'Here's a first complication!' said Jack Ryan, who began to get quite anxious.

Then, without hesitating, superstitious as he was, said 'I will go down though it be blacker in the pit than in the lowest depths of hell!'

And he began to tackle the long series of ladders, which descended into the dark shaft.

In taking this risk, Jack Ryan needed not to have lost any of his former miner's habits, and to know Dochart Pit well. He descended carefully moreover. His foot tested each rung, some of which were worm-eaten. Any false step would have caused a fatal fall, into this void fifteen hundred feet deep. Jack Ryan was therefore counting each of the landings that he was leaving in sequence to reach a lower landing. He knew that his feet would not touch the sole of the pit before he had passed the thirtieth. Once there, he would have no bother, he thought, in finding the cottage, built, as we know, at the extremity of the main tunnel.

Jack Ryan thus arrived at the twenty-sixth landing, and, consequently, two hundred feet, at most, separated him from the bottom.

Here, he lowered his leg to look for the first rung of the twenty-seventh level ladder. But his leg, swinging in the void, found no foothold.

Jack Ryan knelt down on the landing. He tried to grab the end of the ladder with his hand... but in vain.

It was clear that the twenty-seventh ladder was not in its place, and, therefore, must have been removed.

'Old Nick must have passed here!' he said to himself, not without a certain feeling of terror.

Standing up, arms folded, still wanting to break through this impenetrable darkness, Jack Ryan waited. Then it occurred to him that if he could not go down, the residents of the coalmine could not have come up. There was, indeed, no other communication between the surface of the county and the depths of the pit. If this removal of the lower ladders of the Yarrow Shaft had been carried out since his last visit to the cottage, what had become of Simon Ford, his wife, his son and the engineer? James Starr's prolonged absence evidently proved that he had not left the pit since the day that Jack Ryan had met him in the Yarrow Shaft. How, since then, had the cottage been supplied? Surely they had lacked provisions, these unfortunate folk, trapped fifteen hundred feet below the ground?

All these thoughts crossed Jack Ryan's mind. He saw clearly that he could do nothing by himself to get to the cottage. Had there been some malevolence in the fact that the communications had been interrupted? That did not seem unlikely to him. In any case, the magistrates would advise on that, but they had to be informed as soon as possible.

Jack Ryan leant over the landing.

'Harry! Harry!' he cried with his powerful voice.

The echo of Harry's name rebounded several times but died out finally in the furthest depths of the Yarrow Shaft.

Jack Ryan quickly rescaled the upper ladders, and returned to daylight. He did not lose a moment. Without stopping, he returned to Callander station. He only had to wait a few minutes for the passing of the Edinburgh express, and at three o'clock in the afternoon, he presented himself at the residence of the Lord Provost of the capital.

There, his declaration was received. The precise details that he gave left no doubt of their veracity. Sir W Elphiston, President of the Royal Institution, who was not only a colleague, but a particular friend of James Starr, was also informed, and he asked to conduct the searches that were to be made in Dochart Pit without delay. Placed at his disposal were several officers, equipped with lamps, picks, long rope ladders, not forgetting food and cordials. Then, led by Jack Ryan, they all immediately took the road for the Aberfoyle coalmines.

The same evening, Sir W Elphiston, Jack Ryan and the officers arrived at the mouth of the Yarrow Shaft, and they descended to the twenty-sixth landing, on which Jack Ryan had stopped some hours earlier.

The lamps, attached to the end of long ropes, were sent down into the depths of the shaft, and it was possible to observe that the last four ladders were missing. There was no doubt that all communication between the inside and the outside of Dochart Pit had been intentionally broken.

'What are we waiting for, sir?' asked the impatient Jack Ryan.

'Harry! Harry!' he cried with his powerful voice.

'We are waiting for the lamps to be brought back up, my boy,' replied Sir W Elphiston. 'Then, we shall go down to the floor of the last tunnel, and you will lead us...'

'To the cottage,' cried Jack Ryan, 'and, if necessary, to the last depths of the pit!'

As soon as the lamps were pulled up, the officers fixed the rope ladders to the landing, which would roll out into the shaft. The lower landings were still there. They could descend from one to the next.

This was not achieved without great difficulty. Jack Ryan, the first, suspended himself on these swaying ladders, and he was the first to reach the floor of the mine.

Sir W Elphiston and the officers soon joined him.

The roundabout, formed by the bottom of the Yarrow Shaft, was completely deserted, but Sir W Elphiston was not particularly surprised to hear Jack Ryan cry:

'Here are some pieces of the ladders, and they are half-burnt pieces!'

'Burnt!' repeated Sir W Elphiston. Indeed, there were the ashes, long since cooled.

'Do you think, sir,' asked Jack Ryan, 'that the engineer James Starr had an interest in burning these ladders and cutting off all communication with the outside?'

'No,' replied Sir W Elphiston, who remained pensive. 'Let us go to the cottage, my boy! It is there that we shall discover the truth.'

Jack Ryan nodded his head, though he was hardly convinced. But, taking a lamp from the hands of an officer, he quickly advanced through the main tunnel of Dochart Pit.

Everyone followed him.

A quarter of an hour later, Sir W Elphiston and his companions had reached the hollow at the bottom of which Simon Ford's cottage had been built. No light lit the windows.

Jack Ryan hurried towards the door, which he pushed open forcefully.

The cottage was deserted.

They visited the rooms of the dark habitation. No sign of violence inside. Everything was in order, as if old Madge had still been there. The store of supplies was even plentiful, and would have done the Ford family several days.

The absence of the cottage hosts was therefore inexplicable. But could the time they had left the cottage be precisely determined? Yes, for in this environment where day did not succeed night, Madge used to mark each day of her calendar with a cross.

This calendar was hung on the living-room wall. But the last cross that had been made was on the 6th December, that is to say one day after James Starr's arrival – that was what Jack Ryan was in a position to confirm. It was therefore evident that since the 6th December, that is to say, ten days ago, Simon Ford, his wife, his son and his guest had left the cottage. Could a new exploration of the pit, undertaken by the engineer, provide the reason for such a long absence? Evidently not.

So, at least, reasoned Sir W Elphiston. After having meticulously examined the cottage, he was at a loss as to what should be done.

The darkness was profound. The brightness of the lamps, balanced in the officers' hands, only studded these impenetrable shadows.

Suddenly Jack Ryan gave a shout.

'There! There!' he said.

And his finger pointed to a rather bright glow, which was moving in the faraway darkness of the tunnel.

'My friends, let us pursue this light!' replied Sir W Elphiston.

'A brownie's fire!' cried Jack Ryan, 'What's the point? We'll never reach it!'

The President of the Royal Institution and the officers, little disposed to superstition, rushed in the direction indicated by the moving glimmer. Jack Ryan, bravely playing his part, did not remain behind for long.

It was a long and tiring chase. The glowing lantern seemed to be carried by a creature of small size, but singular agility. At every moment this creature disappeared behind some cutting work; then it was spotted again at the end of a transversal tunnel. Quick swerves put it again out of sight. It seemed to have definitively disappeared, when suddenly the glimmer of its lantern threw out a bright beam once again. In short, they made little gain on it, and Jack Ryan persisted in believing, not without reason, that they would never reach it.

For an hour of this hopeless chase, Sir W Elphiston and his companions pressed into the south-west part of Dochart Pit. They too began to wonder if they were not dealing with some uncatchable will o' the wisp.

At that moment, however, it seemed that the distance between the will o' the wisp and those in pursuit decreased. Was it the fatigue of fleeing, or did the creature want to attract Sir W Elphiston and his companions to where the inhabitants of the cottage had perhaps been attracted themselves? It would have been difficult to answer this question.

In any case, the officers, seeing this distance lessen, redoubled their efforts. The glow, which had always shined more than two hundred steps in front of them, was now at less than fifty. This interval diminished further. The bearer of the lantern became more visible. Sometimes, when it turned its head, the vague profile of a human figure could be recognised, and, unless a bogle had assumed this shape, Jack Ryan was forced to admit that it was not a supernatural being.

And so, while running faster, he cried:

'Come on, men! He's tiring! We'll soon get him, and if he speaks as well as he bolts, he will be able to tell us a lot!'

However, the chase became more difficult just then. Indeed, in the area of the furthest depths of the pit, narrow tunnels intersected like the alleys of a labyrinth. In this maze, the lantern-bearer could easily escape the officers. It sufficed for him to put out his lantern and jump to the side into the back of some dark refuge.

'And, yet,' Sir W Elphiston thought, 'if he wants to escape us, why does he not do so?'

This elusive being had not done so thus far; but, just when this thought was crossing Sir W Elphiston's mind, the glow suddenly disappeared, and the officers, continuing their chase, arrived almost immediately in front of a narrow opening in the shale rocks, at the end of a narrow passage.

To slip in there, after turning up the light on their lamps, to cross this mouth which opened up before them, was accomplished by Sir W Elphiston, Jack Ryan and their companions in a matter of moments.

But they had not taken a hundred steps in a new larger and higher tunnel, when they suddenly stopped. There, near to the wall, four bodies were stretched out on the ground – perhaps four corpses!

'James Starr!' said Sir W Elphiston.

'Harry! Harry!' cried Jack Ryan, hurrying to the body of his friend.

It was, indeed, the engineer, Madge, Simon and Harry Ford, who were stretched out there, motionless.

But, then, one of these bodies straightened up, and the exhausted voice of old Madge was heard murmuring these words:

'The others! The others first!'

Sir W Elphiston, Jack Ryan and the officers tried to rouse the engineer and his companions by making them swallow some drops of cordial. They succeeded almost at once. These unfortunate folk, impounded for ten days in New Aberfoyle, were dying of hunger.

And, if they had not succumbed during this long imprisonment – James Starr informed Sir W Elphiston – it was because three times they had found a loaf of bread and a jug of water nearby. No doubt, the benevolent creature to whom they owed their lives had been unable to do more...

Sir W Elphiston wondered if that was not the work of this elusive will o' the wisp, which had just attracted them precisely to the area where James Starr and his companions were lying.

Be that as it may, the engineer, Madge, Simon and Harry Ford were saved. They were taken back to the cottage, passing again by the narrow opening that the lantern-bearer seemed to have wanted to indicate to Sir W Elphiston.

And if James Starr and his companions had not been able to rediscover the mouth of the tunnel that the dynamite had blasted open, it was because this mouth had been solidly blocked by superimposed rocks that in the profound darkness they had been able neither to recognise nor to dismantle.

Thus, while they were exploring the vast crypt, had all communication between old and New Aberfoyle deliberately been severed by an enemy hand!

Four bodies were stretched out on the ground...

CHAPTER THIRTEEN

Coal City

THREE YEARS AFTER the events which have just been recounted, the Joanne or Murray guidebooks were recommending as 'a great attraction' to the numerous tourists who travelled in Stirlingshire, a visit of several hours to the coalmines of New Aberfoyle.

No mine, in any country of the New or Old World, offered a more curious sight.

First, the visitor was transported without danger or effort to the base level of the exploitation, at fifteen hundred feet below the surface of the county.

For, seven miles away, south-west of Callander, a descending tunnel, embellished with a monumental entrance complete with turrets, crenulations and machicolations, opened up. This wide and gently sloping tunnel came to an end directly at the extraordinary crypt hollowed out of the mass of the Scottish ground.

A double railway, the wagons of which were pulled by hydraulic force, served hourly the village that had been established beneath the county, under the perhaps slightly ambitious name of 'Coal City'.

On arrival at Coal City, the visitor found himself in an environment where electricity played a major role as provider of heat and light.

For the ventilation shafts, numerous though they might be, were not able to bring enough daylight to the deep darkness of New Aberfoyle. However, an intense light filled this dark environment, where numerous electric discs replaced the solar disc. Suspended from the intrados of the vaults or hung on natural pillars, all fed by the continuous current produced by the electromagnetic machines – some suns, others stars – they amply illuminated this domain. When the hour of rest came, a switch sufficed to produce night artificially in these deep abysses of the mine.

All this equipment, large or small, operated in a vacuum, that is to say that their luminous arcs never communicated with the ambient air. So that even if the atmosphere had been mixed with firedamp in an explosive proportion, there would have been no fear of explosion. Consequently, the electric power was also invariably used for all the needs of industrial life and domestic life, as much in the houses of Coal City as in the tunnels exploited by New Aberfoyle.

It must be emphasised that the engineer James Starr's predictions concerning the exploitation of the new mine had not been disappointed. The wealth of the coal seams was incalculable. It was in the west of the crypt, a quarter of a mile from Coal City, that the first seams had been attacked by the miners' picks. The work of the pit was directly linked to the surface work by the ventilation and production shafts, which put the various levels of the mine in communication with the ground above. The great tunnel, where the hydraulic-traction railway operated, served only to transport the inhabitants of Coal City.

We recall the singular structure of this vast cavern, where the old overman and his companions had stopped during their first exploration. There, above their heads, curved a gothic pointed dome. The pillars that supported it disappeared into the shale vault, at a height of three hundred feet – a height almost equal to the Mammoth Dome of the Kentucky caves.

We know that this enormous hall – the largest of the whole American hypogeum – can easily contain five thousand people. This part of New Aberfoyle shared the same proportions and layout. But, instead of the admirable stalactites of the famous cave, here the eye fell on the swellings of carboniferous seams, which seemed to burst from all the walls under the pressure of the shale faults. One would have said they were jet-black relief sculptures with specks that sparkled under the rays of the electric discs.

Under this dome stretched a loch comparable in size to the Dead Sea of the Mammoth Cave – a deep loch whose transparent waters teemed with eyeless fish, and which the engineer had named Loch Malcolm.

It was there, in this huge natural hollow that Simon Ford had built his new cottage, and he would not have swapped it for the finest hotel in Princes Street in Edinburgh. This habitation was situated on the edge of the lake, and its five windows opened onto the dark waters, which extended beyond the eye's limit.

Two months later, a second dwelling was erected neighbouring Simon Ford's cottage. It belonged to James Starr. The engineer had given body and soul to New Aberfoyle. He, too, had wanted to live here, and for him to consent to go back up to the world outside, there had to be very pressing considerations. Here, he was living in the very middle of his world of miners.

Since the discovery of the new deposits, all the workers of the old colliery had hurried to leave the plough and harrow to work again with the pick and mattock. Attracted by the certainty that they would never lack work and tempted by the high pay that the prosperity of the exploitation was going to allocate to the workforce, they had deserted the soil in droves in favour of the underground, and they were accommodated in the mine itself, which lent itself naturally to this inhabitation.

These miners' houses were built in brick and dotted around in a picturesque fashion, some on the banks of Loch Malcolm, others under the arches, which seemed made for resisting the weight of the vaults like the buttresses of a cathedral. Hewers who broke the rock, putters who transported the coal, foremen, timbermen who shored up the tunnels, roadmen to whom the maintenance of the roadways was allocated, infillers, who substitute stone for coal in the excavated parts, in short, all the workers who were specifically employed in the underground work, made their home in New Aberfoyle and gradually founded Coal City, situated under the eastern end of Loch Katrine, in north Stirlingshire.

These miners' houses were built in brick...

It was a sort of Flemish village that rose up on the banks of Loch Malcolm. A chapel, dedicated to St Giles, dominated this whole complex from the height of an enormous rock, the foot of which bathed in the waters of this subterranean sea.

When this underground city was lit up with the bright lights projected from the discs suspended from the pillars of the dome or from the arches of the naves, it presented a rather fantastical sight, with an uncanny effect, which justified the Joanne and Murray guidebooks' recommendation. That was why visitors flocked there.

That the inhabitants of Coal City were proud of their settlement went without saying. Consequently they only rarely left the workers' city, following in that respect Simon Ford, who never wanted to leave it. The old overman claimed that it always rained 'up there', and given the climate of the United Kingdom, it must be admitted that he was not entirely wrong. And so the families of New Aberfoyle prospered. They had attained a certain comfort these last three years that they had never managed to obtain at the surface of the county. Many babies, who were born after operations had been resumed, had never breathed the outside air.

So Jack Ryan could say, 'It's been eighteen months since they stopped feeding at their mothers' breast, and yet, they have never seen the light of day!'

It should be noted, in this respect, that one of the first to respond to the engineer's call had been Jack Ryan. This joyful fellow had made it his duty to resume his former occupation. Melrose Farm had therefore lost its usual singer and piper. But that is not to say that Jack Ryan sang no more. Quite the contrary – and the echoes of New Aberfoyle used their stone lungs to answer to him.

Jack Ryan had moved into Simon Ford's new cottage. He had been offered a room which he had accepted without fuss, being the simple and frank man that he was. Old Madge loved him for his good character and fine humour. She shared ever so slightly his ideas on the subject of the fantastical beings that must haunt the mine, and the two of them, when they were alone, told each other stories to send shivers down the spine, stories well worthy of enriching the mythology of the far north.

Jack Ryan thus became the delight of the cottage. He was, besides, a good person and a solid worker. Six months after the resumption of operations, he was the head of a team of pit workers.

'A good job well done, Mr Ford,' he was saying, a few days after he had moved in. 'You have found a new seam, and, since you haven't, after all, had to pay for it with your life, it hasn't been too expensive!'

'No, Jack, we've got ourselves quite a bargain!' replied the old overman. 'But neither Mr Starr, nor myself, have forgotten that we owe our lives to you!'

'But no,' rejoined Jack Ryan. 'It's owed to your son Harry, because he had the good idea of accepting my invitation to the Irvine festival...'

'And not to go, isn't that right?' responded Harry, shaking his friend's hand. 'No, Jack, it's owed to you, barely recovered from your injuries, to you who wasted not a day, nor an hour, that we owe being found alive in the mine!'

'Well, no!' retaliated the stubborn lad. 'I won't let things be said that aren't true! I was able to hurry to find out what had become of you, Harry, and that's all. But, to give everyone their due, I would add that without that elusive bogle...'

'Ah! There we are!' cried Simon Ford. 'A bogle!'

'A bogle, a brownie, a son of a fairy,' repeated Jack Ryan, 'a fire-maiden's grandson, an Urisk, in short whatever you like! But it is no less certain that without it, we would have never gone into the tunnel from which you could not get out!'

'Without a doubt, Jack,' replied Harry. 'It remains to be seen whether this being is as supernatural as you want to believe.'

'Supernatural!' cried Jack Ryan. 'But it is as supernatural as a will o' the wisp that you see running lantern in hand, that you want to catch, that escapes you like a sylph, that vanishes like a shadow! Be assured, Harry, we'll see it again one day or another!'

'Well Jack,' said Simon Ford, 'fairy or not, we shall try to find it, and you must help us in that.'

'You'll be looking for trouble, Mr Ford!' replied Jack Ryan.

'Good! Let it come, Jack!'

We can easily imagine the extent to which the domain of New Aberfoyle soon became familiar to the members of the Ford Family, and more particularly to Harry. He came to know its most secret turns. He was even able to say which point of the surface of the ground corresponded to such and such a point of the mine. He knew that above this layer flowed the Firth of Clyde, that there stretched Loch Lomond or Loch Katrine. These pillars were a buttress of the hills of the Trossachs which they supported. This vault formed a basement to Dumbarton. Above this large pond passed the Balloch railway. There ended the Scottish coast. There began the sea, whose crashing waves could be distinctly heard during the great equinoctial storms. Harry would have been a marvellous tour leader of these natural catacombs, and what the Alpine guides do on the snowy peaks, in broad daylight, he could have done in the shadowy world of the mine, with an incomparably reliable instinct.

Consequently, he loved this New Aberfoyle. So that sometimes, lamp on hat, he adventured to its furthest depths. He explored its ponds on a boat that he skilfully manoeuvred. He even went hunting, for numerous wild birds had been introduced into the crypt – pintail ducks, snipes, scoters – which fed on the fish that swarmed in these black waters. It seemed that Harry's eyes were made for dark spaces, like the eyes of a sailor are for distant horizons.

But, wandering thus, Harry was irresistibly led on by the hope of rediscovering the mysterious creature whose intervention, if truth be told, had played a larger part than any other in saving him and his family. Would he succeed? Yes, it was not to be doubted, if he believed his presentiments. No, if he had to draw a conclusion from the little success that his searches had had thus far.

As for the attacks directed against the old overman's family before the discovery of New Aberfoyle, they had not been renewed.

This was the state of affairs in this strange domain.

It must not be imagined that, even at this period when the outlines of Coal City had been barely drawn, all entertainment was absent from the subterranean town, and that life was monotonous.

It was nothing of the sort. The population, having the same interests, the same tastes and more or less the same income, constituted to all intents and purposes one large family. They knew one other, mixed with one another, and the need to go and look for pleasures above ground was seldom felt.

Moreover, every Sunday, walks in the mine, excursion on the lochs and ponds were just as agreeable distractions.

Often too, you could hear the sounds of the bagpipes resounding on the banks of Loch Malcolm. The Scots gathered at the call of their national instrument. They would dance, and on that day, Jack Ryan, dressed in Highland costume, was king of the festivities.

In short, the result of all this, in Simon Ford's view, was that Coal City could already rival the Scottish capital, a city subjected to the cold of winter, the heat of summer, a detestably intemperate climate, and which, with its atmosphere poisoned by the smoke of its factories, justified all too accurately its nickname of Auld Reekie.[12]

---

[12] Auld Reekie, nickname given to old Edinburgh.

They would dance on the banks of Loch Malcolm.

CHAPTER FOURTEEN

Hanging by a Thread

IN SUCH CONDITIONS, with its dearest desires fulfilled, Simon Ford's family was happy. However, it could be observed that Harry, who already had a rather gloomy character, was more and more 'inside himself', as Madge put it. Jack Ryan, despite his good humour, and being himself so communicative, was unable to bring him 'out of himself.'

One Sunday, in the month of June, the two friends were walking on the banks of Loch Malcolm. Coal City was sleepy. Outside the weather was stormy. Violent rains produced a warm mist from the earth. One could not breathe properly in the county above ground.

In Coal City, by contrast, there was absolute calm, a mild temperature, and neither rain nor wind. Nothing of the battle with the elements outside was experienced there. Consequently, a certain number of walkers from Stirling and its surroundings had come to take a little fresh air in the depths of the mine.

The electric discs emitted a beam that would have surely been the envy of the British sun, more screened by clouds than is desirable for a Sunday sun.

Jack Ryan remarked on this lively throng of visitors to his friend Harry. But the latter did not appear to pay these words even the slightest attention.

'Look, Harry!' cried Jack Ryan. 'How eager they are to come and see us! Come on, my friend! Chase your sad ideas away a little to do the honours to our place here! You would make all these folk from above think that we could envy their lot.'

'Jack,' replied Harry, 'don't bother about me! You are cheerful enough for two!'

'Old Nick take me,' retorted Jack Ryan, 'if your melancholy

doesn't finish by rubbing off on me! My eyes are dull, my lips are shut, laughter remains in the bottom of my throat, my memory for songs deserts me! Come on, Harry, what's up?'

'You know, Jack.'

'Always the same thought?'

'Always.'

'Ah, poor Harry!' replied Jack Ryan, shrugging his shoulders, 'if, like me, you would put all that down to the bogles of the mine, you would have more peace of mind!'

'You know very well, Jack, that the bogles only exist in your imagination, and that, since the resumption of operations, not one has been seen again in New Aberfoyle.'

'That may be so, Harry! But, if the brownies are no longer showing themselves, it seems to me that those you want to blame for all those extraordinary things are not showing themselves either!'

'I shall find them, Jack!'

'Oh, Harry, Harry! The sprites of New Aberfoyle are not easy to discover!'

'I'll find them, your supposed sprites!' replied Harry in a tone of the most energetic conviction.

'So, you mean to punish...'

'Punish and reward, Jack. If one hand imprisoned us in that tunnel, I haven't forgotten that another hand saved us! No, I haven't forgotten that!'

'Oh! Harry!' replied Jack Ryan, 'Are you so sure that the two hands don't belong to the same body?'

'Why, Jack? Where do you get that idea from?'

'Fire-maid... you know... Harry. These creatures, that live in pits...they don't behave like us!'

'They are made like us, Jack!'

'No, Harry... no... Besides, you can't imagine that a madman has managed to introduce himself...'

'A madman!' replied Harry, 'A madman who could have such a succession of ideas! A madman, this criminal who, from the day that he broke the ladders of the Yarrow Shaft, hasn't stopped causing us injury!'

'But he isn't doing it any more, Harry. For three years, no malicious act has been committed either against you or your family!'

'It doesn't matter, Jack,' replied Harry. 'I have the feeling that this wicked being, whatever it is, hasn't renounced his projects. I couldn't say what grounds I have for saying this. But, Jack, in the interest of the new exploitation, I want to know who he is and where he comes from.'

'In the interest of the new exploitation...?' asked Jack Ryan, rather surprised.

'Yes, Jack,' resumed Harry. 'I don't know if I'm deluding myself, but I see in this whole business an interest contrary to ours. I have often thought about it, and I don't believe that I'm mistaken. Remember the series of inexplicable facts, which led logically from one to the next. The anonymous letter, contradicting my father's, proves above all that a human had knowledge about our projects and wanted to prevent them being realised. Mr Starr came to visit us at Dochart Pit. I had hardly taken him in there when an enormous stone was thrown at us, and all communication was immediately cut off by the breaking of the Yarrow Shaft ladders. Our exploration began. An experiment, which ought to reveal the existence of a new seam, was then rendered impossible by the blocking of the cracks in the shale. Nevertheless, the observations were made and the seam was found. We retraced our steps. A great breeze was produced in the air. Our lamp broke. Darkness surrounded us. We succeeded, however, in following the dark tunnel... There was no longer a way out. The mouth was blocked. We were imprisoned. Well, Jack, don't you see a criminal mind in all that? Yes! A being, elusive up until now, but not supernatural, as you persist in believing, was hidden in the mine. For some reason that I cannot understand, he was trying to deny us access. He was there! ... A feeling tells me that he is still there, and who knows if he isn't planning some terrible strike! Well, Jack, I will find him if I have to risk my life doing it!'

Harry had spoken with a conviction that seriously shook his friend.

Jack Ryan sensed that Harry was indeed right – at least about the past. Whether or not these extraordinary facts had a natural or supernatural cause, they were no less clear.

However, the brave lad did not renounce his way of explaining these events. But, realising that Harry would never admit the intervention of a mysterious sprite, he fell back on the incident that seemed irreconcilable with the malevolence directed against the Ford family.

'Well, Harry,' he said, 'if I am obliged to concede to you on a certain number of points, don't you think like me that some benevolent brownie, bringing you bread and water, could have saved your...'

'Jack,' replied Harry interrupting him, 'the helpful being, whom you want to turn into a supernatural creature, exists as tangibly as the criminal in question, and I will seek both of them as far as the furthest depths of the mine.'

'But do you have some clue to guide you in your searches?' asked Jack Ryan.

'Perhaps,' replied Harry. 'Listen carefully. Five miles to the west of New Aberfoyle, under the portion of the rock mass that supports Ben Lomond, there is a natural shaft that descends perpendicularly into the very bowels of the seam. Eight days ago, I wanted to test its depth. Now, while my sounding line was descending and I was leaning over the mouth of the shaft, the air seemed to me to be moving inside, as if it was being beaten by a great flapping of wings.

'It was probably some bird gone astray in the lower tunnels of the mine,' replied Jack.

'That's not all, Jack,' resumed Harry. 'This very morning I returned to this shaft, and there, putting my ear to it, I believe I heard a sort of groaning...'

Five miles to the west... there is a natural shaft...

'Groaning!' cried Jack. 'You are mistaken, Harry! It was a current of air... unless a bogle...'

'Tomorrow, Jack,' continued Harry, 'I will know what to believe.'

'Tomorrow?' replied Jack looking at his friend.

'Yes, tomorrow I shall descend into this pit.'

'Harry, that's tempting Providence, that is!'

'No, Jack, for I will ask for His help in descending there. Tomorrow, we shall both go to the shaft with some of our comrades. A long rope, to which I shall attach myself, will enable you to lower me down and to pull me back up on an agreed signal. Can I count on you, Jack?'

'Harry,' replied Jack Ryan shaking his head, 'I will do what you ask of me, and yet, I repeat, you are wrong.'

'Better to do it and be wrong than to regret not having done it,' said Harry in a decided tone. 'So, tomorrow morning, at six o' clock, and not another word! Goodbye, Jack!'

And, so as not to continue a conversation in which Jack Ryan would again try to fight against his plans, Harry abruptly left his friend and returned to the cottage.

It must be admitted, however, that Jack's apprehensions were not exaggerated. If some personal enemy threatened Harry, if he was to be found at the bottom of this shaft where the young miner was going to look for him, Harry would be exposed. But what were the chances of him admitting that this was so?

'And, anyway,' repeated Jack Ryan, 'why give himself so much bother in explaining a series of facts that are explained so readily by the supernatural intervention of the sprites of the mine?'

Be that as it may, the next day, Jack Ryan and three miners from his team accompanied Harry to the mouth of the suspicious shaft.

Harry had said nothing of his plan to either James Starr or to the old overman. On his side, Jack Ryan had been discreet enough not to speak of it. The other miners, seeing them leave, had thought that they were embarking on nothing more than a simple exploration of the seam, following its vertical cross section.

Harry was equipped with a two hundred foot long rope. This rope was not thick, but it was solid. Harry did not have to descend or remount by the force of his hands, the rope had only to be strong enough to support his weight. It was his companions who had the task of letting him slide into the chasm, and then pulling him out. A tug of the rope would serve as signal between him and them.

The shaft was quite wide, about twelve feet in diameter at the mouth. A beam was placed across it, like a bridge, so that the rope, sliding on its surface, could maintain its axis in the shaft. This was a vital precaution so that Harry would not hit the side walls during the descent.

Harry was ready.

'Do you persist in your project of exploring this pit?' Jack Ryan asked him in a low voice.

The rope was first attached around Harry's back, then under his arms, so that his body could not tip over.

Supported thus, Harry had his two hands free. At his belt, he hung a safety lamp and one of those large Scottish knives, which are carried in a leather sheath.

Harry advanced to the middle of the beam, around which the cord was passed.

Then, his companions let him slide down and he sunk slowly into the shaft. As the rope gently spun round, the glow of his lamp fell successively on each point of the walls, and Harry was able to examine them carefully.

The walls were made of coal-bearing shale. They were too smooth for him to be able to haul himself up on their surface.

Harry reckoned that he was descending at a moderate speed – about a foot per second. He was therefore able to see clearly, and to be poised for every eventuality.

After two minutes, that is to say a depth of about one

hundred and twenty feet, the descent had passed without incident. There was no lateral passage in the wall of the shaft, which
was gradually narrowing into a tunnel. But Harry began to feel
a fresher air, which was coming from below – from which he
concluded that the lower extremity of the shaft communicated
with some passage of a lower level of the crypt.

The cord was still sliding. The darkness was absolute. The
silence, absolute too. If a living being, whatever it might be, had
sought refuge in this mysterious and deep abyss, then either it
was not there, or no movement betrayed its presence.

Harry, increasingly defiant as he descended, had pulled the
knife from its sheath, and he held it in his right hand.

At a depth of one hundred and eighty feet, Harry sensed that
he had reached the bottom, for the rope relaxed and unrolled no
longer.

Harry breathed for a moment. One of his fears had not been
realised, that is to say, that during his descent the rope would be
cut above him. He had not, moreover, noticed any crevice in the
walls that could conceal some creature or other.

The lower extremity of the shaft was greatly narrowed.

Harry detached the lamp from his belt and moved it over the
ground. He had not been mistaken in his conjectures.

A narrow passageway was sunk into the side below the seam.
He would have to stoop to enter it, and drag himself on his
hands to follow it.

Harry wanted to see in which direction this tunnel branched
off, and if it ended at a pit.

He got down on the ground and began to crawl. But an
obstacle stopped him almost immediately.

In touching it, he thought that this obstacle felt like a body
that was blocking the passage.

Harry first recoiled with a sharp feeling of repulsion, then he
returned.

His senses had not deceived him. What had stopped him was
indeed a body. He grabbed it, and realised that, though frozen

at the extremities, it was not yet completely cold.

To hold it to himself, bring it to the bottom of the shaft, shine the light of his lamp on it – this was done faster than it could be said.

'A child!' cried Harry.

The child, found at the bottom of this abyss, was still breathing, but its breath was so faint that Harry believed that it might stop. He had to, therefore, without wasting a moment's time, bring this poor little creature back up to the mouth of the shaft and then to the cottage where Madge would lavish her care.

Harry, forgetting all other preoccupation, readjusted the rope at his belt, attached his lamp to it, held the child with his left arm against his breast, and keeping his right arm free and armed, made the agreed signal so that the rope would be gently hauled in.

The rope tightened, and the ascent began smoothly.

Harry looked around with redoubled attention. He was no longer the only one who was vulnerable.

All went well for the first minutes of the ascent – nothing seemed to be about to happen – when Harry thought he heard a powerful breath that disturbed the layers of air in the depths of the shaft. He looked below, and saw in the darkness a gradually rising mass, which skimmed him in passing.

It was an enormous bird, whose species he could not recognise, and which rose with great beatings of its wings.

The monstrous flying creature stopped, glided for an instant, then turned on Harry with ferocious determination.

Harry had only his right arm to parry the blows of the beast's formidable beak.

Harry defended himself thus, while protecting the child as best he could. But it was not the child, but himself that the bird was attacking. Impeded by the rotation of the rope, he could not mortally wound it.

The struggle continued. Harry cried out with the full force of his lungs, hoping that his cries would be heard from above.

'A child!' cried Harry.

133

Harry defended himself thus, while protecting the child...

It must have worked, because the rope was immediately hoisted more quickly.

There was still a height of eighty feet to go. The bird then leaped more violently on Harry. With a blow of his knife he injured its wing; the bird, emitting a harsh squawk, disappeared into the depths of the shaft.

But – terrible situation – Harry, brandishing his knife to strike the bird, had sliced into the rope, a strand of which was now cut.

Harry's hair stood on end.

The rope was giving way little by little, at more than a hundred feet from the bottom of the pit...!

Harry gave out a desperate cry.

A second strand broke under the double weight that the half-cut rope was bearing.

Harry let go of his knife and, in a superhuman effort, just when the rope was about to break, he managed to seize the part above with his right hand. But, although he had an iron grip, he felt the rope gradually slip through his fingers.

He would have been able to grab the rope with two hands, in sacrificing the child that he bore in his arms... He did not even want to think of it.

However, Jack Ryan and his companions, perturbed by Harry's cries, were hauling the rope more energetically.

Harry did not think that he would be able to hold on until he was back up to the mouth of the shaft. His face crumpled. He closed his eyes for a moment, waiting to fall into the abyss, then he reopened them...

But, at the moment when he was about to release the rope, which he was holding only by its very tip, he was seized and placed on the ground with the child.

The effort then took its toll, and Harry collapsed unconscious into the arms of his comrades.

CHAPTER FIFTEEN

Nell at the Cottage

TWO HOURS LATER, Harry, who had not immediately recovered his senses, and the child, whose weakness was extreme, reached the cottage with the help of Jack Ryan and his companions.

There, these events were recounted to the old overman, and Madge gave all her attention to the poor creature whom her son had just rescued.

Harry had thought that he had taken out a child from the abyss... But it was a girl of fifteen or sixteen. Her vague expression, full of astonishment, her thin figure, attenuated by suffering, her blonde complexion that the light never seemed to have bathed, her frail condition and small size, all made for a being at once bizarre and charming. Jack Ryan, with some justification, compared her to an elf of rather supernatural appearance. Because of the particular circumstances and exceptional environment in which this young girl appeared to have lived until now, she seemed only half to belong to humanity. Her physiognomy was strange. Her eyes, which the brightness of the cottage lamps seemed to tire, looked around in confusion as if everything was new to them.

To this singular being, now lying on Madge's bed and who had just come back to life as if from a deep sleep, the old Scotswoman addressed first these words:

'What's your name?'

'Nell,'[13] replied the girl.

'Nell,' resumed Madge, 'are you in pain?'

'I'm hungry,' replied Nell. 'I haven't eaten since... since...'

[13] Nell is an abbreviation of Helena.

Nell

From these few words she had just pronounced, it was clear that Nell was not used to speaking. The language which she used was old Gaelic, which Simon Ford and his family often used.

At the girl's response, Madge immediately brought her some food. Nell was dying of hunger. How long had she been at the bottom of that shaft? One could not say.

'How many days did you spend there, my lass?' asked Madge.

Nell did not reply. She did not seem to understand the question that had been put to her.

'Since how many days?' resumed Madge.

'Days...?' replied Nell, for whom this word seemed to be lacking all meaning.

Then she shook her head like someone who did not understand what she was being asked.

Madge had taken Nell's hand and was stroking it to give her confidence.

'How old are you, my lass?' she asked, looking at her with kind and reassuring eyes.

The same negative sign from Nell.

'Yes, yes,' resumed Madge, 'how many years?'

'Years?' replied Nell.

And this word, seemed to have no more significance for the young girl than the word 'day'.

Simon Ford, Harry, Jack Ryan and his companions were looking at her with a double feeling of pity and sympathy. The state of this poor creature, dressed in a miserable tunic of coarse material, deeply moved them.

Harry, more than any other, felt irresistibly attracted by Nell's very strangeness.

He approached. He took in his hand the hand that Madge had just released. He looked straight at Nell, whose lips formed a sort of smile, and said to her:

'Nell... there... in the mine... were you alone?'

'Alone! Alone!' cried the young girl, sitting up.

Her expression showed abject horror. Her eyes, which had softened under the young man's expression, became wild again.

'Alone! Alone!' she repeated, and she fell back on to Madge's bed, as if she utterly lacked strength.

'The poor child is still too weak to talk to us,' said Madge, after having tucked in the young girl again. 'A few hours rest and some good food will restore her energy. Come, Simon! Come, Harry! Everyone come away, and let's let sleep do its work!'

On Madge's advice, Nell was left alone, and we can be sure that, an instant later, she was sound asleep.

The event caused quite a stir, not only in the colliery, but also in Stirlingshire, and soon afterwards, in the whole of the United Kingdom. The renown of the strange character of Nell grew. Had a girl been discovered encased in shale rock, like one of those prehistoric creatures that are released from their stone casings by the blow of a pick, there would not have been more fuss.

Without knowing it, Nell became very much the news of the moment. Superstitious folk found here a new text for their story-telling. They readily believed that Nell was the sprite of New Aberfolye, and when Jack Ryan said this to his friend Harry:

'Be that as it may,' replied the young man, 'be that as it may, Jack! But in any case, she's the good sprite! She's the one who saved us, who brought us the bread and water, when we were imprisoned in the mine! She could only be that one! As for the evil sprite, if it's still in the mine, we shall have to find it one day!'

As we can imagine, the engineer James Starr had been the first to hear about what had happened.

Having recovered her strength by the day after her arrival in the cottage, the girl was questioned by him with the greatest concern. She seemed to him to be ignorant of most of the things of life. However, she was intelligent – that much could be seen – but she lacked certain elementary notions: of time, among other things. It was clear that she was not used to dividing time either by hours or by days, and that these very words were unknown to her. Moreover, her eyes, accustomed to the night, operated with difficulty in the brightness of the electric discs; but in the darkness, her sight had an extraordinary sharpness, and her widely dilated pupils enabled her to see into the midst of the deepest shadows. It was also noted that her brain had never received any impressions of the outside world, that no horizon other than that of the mine had spread before her eyes, that for her all of humankind had been contained in this dark crypt. Did she know, the poor girl, that there was a sun and stars, towns and countryside, and a universe in which worlds abounded? It had to be doubted, at least until the day when certain words that she did not yet know would gain a precise meaning for her.

As for the question of knowing whether Nell lived alone in the depths of New Aberfoyle, James Starr had to give up looking for an answer. Every allusion to the subject threw the strange creature into a state of terror. Nell either could not, or would not reply; but there was certainly some secret there, which she might have revealed.

'Do you want to stay with us? Or do you want to return to where you were?' James Starr had asked her.

To the first of these two questions the girl had said, 'Oh yes!' To the second, she had replied only with a cry of terror, then nothing more.

Confronted with this obstinate silence, James Starr, and with him Simon and Harry Ford, did not let their apprehension show. They could not forget the inexplicable facts that had accompanied the discovery of the mine. For although there had been no new incident for three years, they were constantly expecting some new aggression on the part of their invisible enemy. Consequently, they wanted to explore the mysterious shaft. This they did, well-armed and well-accompanied. But they found nothing suspicious. The shaft communicated with the lower floors of the crypt, hollowed into the coal-bearing layer.

James Starr, Simon and Harry often talked about these matters. If one or more criminal beings were hidden in the mine and if they were preparing some trap, Nell would have perhaps been able to tell them, but she was not talking. The least allusion to the young girl's past provoked fits, and it seemed best not to insist. With time, her secret would no doubt come out.

A fortnight after her arrival at the cottage, Nell had become old Madge's most intelligent and zealous helper. Evidently, it seemed entirely natural to her never to leave this house, where she had been so charitably received, and perhaps she did not even imagine that from now on she could live elsewhere. The Ford family was enough for her, and it goes without saying that in the thoughts of these good people, from the moment that Nell entered into the cottage, she had become their adopted child.

Nell was, in truth, charming. Her new life became her. They were no doubt the first happy days of her life. She was full of gratitude to those to whom she owed them. Madge was overcome by an entirely maternal sympathy for Nell. The old overman was soon taken by her in turn. Everyone loved her. Their friend Jack Ryan regretted just one thing: not to have saved her himself. He was often at the cottage. He sang, and Nell, who had never heard singing, found it extremely beautiful; but one could see that the young girl preferred the more serious talks with Harry, who gradually taught her what she did not know about the outside world, to the songs of Jack Ryan.

It must be said that since Nell had appeared in human form, Jack Ryan found himself forced to admit that his belief in bogles was to a certain extent waning. Furthermore, two months later, his superstition received a new blow.

For around this time, Harry made a quite unexpected discovery, which explained in part the appearance of the fire-maidens in the ruins of Dundonald Castle in Irvine.

One day, after a long exploration of the southern part of the mine – an exploration which had lasted several days along the furthest tunnels of this enormous substructure – Harry had with some difficulty climbed a narrow tunnel, formed by a gap in the shale rock. Suddenly, he was very surprised to find himself in the open air. The tunnel had risen diagonally to ground level and ended right in the ruins of Dundonald Castle. There was, therefore, a secret communication between New Aberfoyle and the hill, which was crowned by the old castle. The upper mouth of this tunnel had been impossible to find from the outside, so hidden was it by stones and undergrowth. Consequently, during the enquiry, the magistrates had been unable to discover it.

Several days later, James Starr, led by Harry, came to discover this natural feature of the seam for himself.

'Here,' he said, 'is something to convince these superstitious folk of the mine. Farewell, brownies, bogles and fire-maidens!'

'I don't believe, Mr Starr,' replied Harry, 'that we should be too quick to congratulate ourselves! Their replacements will not be any better, and assuredly could be worse!'

'Indeed, Harry,' replied the engineer, 'but what can we do? Obviously, whatever they are, the beings that hide in the mine communicate with the ground through this tunnel. It was doubtless they who, torch in hand, attracted the *Motala* to the coast, and like the wreckers of yore would have taken the spoils, had Jack Ryan and his companions not happened to be there! Be that as it may, finally everything is explained. Here is the mouth of the den! As for those who were inhabiting it, do they inhabit it still?'

'Yes, because Nell trembles, when we speak to her of it!' replied Harry with conviction. 'Yes, because Nell doesn't want, or doesn't dare to speak of it!'

Harry must have been right. If the mysterious hosts of the mine had abandoned it, or if they were dead, what reason had the girl for keeping quiet?

However, James Starr was absolutely determined to get to the bottom of this secret. He sensed that the future of the new exploitation could depend on it. Therefore the most strict precautions were again taken. The magistrates were informed. Officers secretly occupied the ruins of Dundonald Castle. Harry himself hid, for several nights, in the middle of the undergrowth which bristled on the hill. A vain effort. Nothing was discovered. No human being crossed the opening.

Soon it was concluded that the criminals had definitively left New Aberfoyle, and that, as far as Nell was concerned, they believed her to be dead at the bottom of the shaft where she had been abandoned. Before the exploitation, the mine could offer them a safe refuge, hidden from all enquiries. But since then things had changed. The refuge had become difficult to hide. It could reasonably have been hoped that there was nothing more to fear for the future. However, James Starr was not absolutely reassured. Neither could Harry surrender, and he often repeated, 'Nell was clearly mixed up in all this mystery. If she had nothing more to fear, why should she keep quiet? It cannot be doubted that she is happy to be with us. She loves us all. She adores my mother. If she is silent about her past, about what might reassure us for the future, she must have some terrible secret weighing on her that her conscience prevents her from revealing! Perhaps then, she believes it in our interest more than in her own that she should withdraw herself into this inexplicable silence!'

It was in consequence of these various considerations that, by common agreement, it had been decided that all conversation that might remind the young girl of her past should be avoided.

One day, however, Harry made known to Nell what James Starr, his father and mother, and he himself believed that they owed to her intervention.

It was a holiday. Workers were as idle in the subterranean domain as on the surface of Stirlingshire. People were going for walks more or less everywhere. Songs resounded in a score of places under the sonorous vaults of New Aberfoyle.

Harry and Nell had left the cottage and were slowly following the left bank of Loch Malcolm. There, the electric glares fell with less violence, and their beams broke capriciously on the angles of picturesque rocks that supported the dome. This half-light better suited Nell's eyes, which grew accustomed to the light only with considerable difficulty.

After an hour of walking, Harry and his companion stopped opposite St Giles' Chapel, on a sort of natural terrace that dominated the waters of the loch.

'Your eyes are still not used to the day, Nell,' said Harry, 'and certainly, they couldn't bear the light of the sun.'

'No, without doubt not,' replied the girl, 'if the sun is as you have pictured it for me, Harry.'

'Nell,' resumed Harry, 'I couldn't give you a fair idea of its splendour nor of the beauties of this world that your eyes have never observed just through words. But, tell me, can it be that since the day you were born in the depths of the mine, can it be that you have never climbed up to the surface of the ground?'

'Never, Harry,' replied Nell, 'and I don't think that, even as a little girl, either a father or a mother carried me there. I would have surely kept some memory of the outside!'

'I believe so,' replied Harry. 'Besides, at that time Nell, there were many other than you who had never left the mine. Communications with the outside were difficult and I knew more than one lad or lass who, at your age, were still ignorant of all the things that are unknown to you up there! But now, the railway of the great tunnel takes us to the surface of the county in a matter of minutes. So I can't wait, Nell, to hear you say, "Come, Harry, my eyes can bear the light of day, and I want to see the sun! I want to see God's work!"'

'I will say it to you, Harry' replied the girl, 'before long, I hope. I will go and admire with you this outside world, and yet...'

'What do you want to say, Nell?' asked Harry eagerly. 'Would you have some regret in abandoning the dark pit in which you have lived for these first years of your life, and from which we brought you out nearly dead?'

'No, Harry,' replied Nell. 'I was only thinking that the shadows are beautiful too. If you knew all that eyes used to their depth can see! There are shadows that pass and that you love to follow in their flight! Sometimes these are circles, which intersect before your eyes and from which you don't want to come out! At the bottom of the mine there are black holes, full of hazy lights. And then, you hear noises that speak to you! You see, Harry, you have to have lived there to understand what I feel, what I can't express to you!'

'And were you not afraid, Nell, when you were alone?'

'Harry,' replied the young girl, 'it was when I was alone that I wasn't afraid!'

Nell's voice changed slightly in pronouncing these words. Harry, however, believed he should press her a little, and said:

'But you could get lost in these long tunnels, Nell. Weren't you fearful then of losing your way?'

'No, Harry. I have known, since way back, all the twists and turns of the new mine!'

'Did you not go out of it, sometimes...?'

'Yes... sometimes...' replied the young girl hesitantly, 'sometimes I came into the old Aberfoyle mine.'

'Did you know the old cottage then?'

'The cottage... yes... but those who inhabited it, only from a distance!'

'It was my father and mother,' replied Harry, 'and me! We wanted never to abandon our former abode!'

'Perhaps that would have been better for you all...!' murmured the young girl.

'But why, Nell? Wasn't it our obstinacy in not leaving it, which made us discover the new seam? And hasn't this discovery had happy consequences for an entire population which has recovered here its comfort through the work, and for you, Nell, who, restored to life, has found love from all around you!'

'For me!' replied Nell eagerly, 'Yes! Whatever happens! For the others... who knows?'

'What do you mean?'

'Nothing... nothing! ... But, it was dangerous to break into the new mine! Yes! Very dangerous! Harry! One day, careless people penetrated into these abysses. They were far, very far! They got lost...'

'Lost?' said Harry looking at Nell.

'Yes... lost...' replied Nell, whose voice was trembling. 'Their lamp went out! They couldn't find their way...'

'And there,' cried Harry, 'imprisoned for eight long days, Nell, they were close to dying! And without a kind person, that God sent them, an angel perhaps, who secretly brought them a bit of food, without a mysterious guide who later led their liberators to them, they would never have got out of that tomb!'

'And how do you know that?' asked the young girl.

'Because these men were James Starr... my father... and me, Nell!'

Nell, raising her head, grabbed the young man's hand, and she looked at him with such fixity that he felt troubled down to the very depths of his heart.

'You!' repeated the young girl.

'Yes!' replied Harry, after a moment of silence, 'and the person to whom we owe our lives is you, Nell! It could only have been you!'

Nell let her head fall between her two hands, without replying. Never had Harry seen her so deeply upset.

'Those who saved you, Nell,' he added in an emotional voice, 'already owed you their lives, and do you think they can ever forget that?'

'You!' repeated the young girl.

CHAPTER SIXTEEN

On the Winding Ladder

MEANWHILE, THE EXPLOITATION works of New Aberfoyle were being conducted to great profit. It goes without saying that the engineer James Starr and Simon Ford – the first discoverers of this rich coal basin – shared largely in its profits. Harry therefore became a good match. But he hardly thought about leaving the cottage. He had replaced his father in the functions of overman and he assiduously watched over this whole world of miners.

Jack Ryan was proud and delighted with all the good fortune that came to his friend. He too, was doing well. The two of them saw each other often, either in the cottage, or at the coal-face. Jack Ryan was not oblivious to the feelings that Harry showed for the girl. Harry would not admit it, but Jack laughed out loud when his friend shook his head in denial.

It must be said that one of Jack Ryan's deepest wishes was to accompany Nell to the county's surface. He wanted to see her astonishment, her admiration before this nature as yet unknown to her. He really hoped that Harry would bring him along during this excursion. Until then, however, his friend had never made the proposition – which continued to concern him somewhat.

One day, Jack Ryan was descending one of the ventilation shafts by which the lower levels of the mine communicated with the ground above. He had taken one of those ladders, which by rising and descending in successive windings, allows men to go up and down without tiring. Twenty windings of the machine had lowered him about five hundred feet, when on the narrow landing onto which he had stepped, he met Harry, who was climbing up to the surface work.

'Is that you?' said Jack, looking at his companion, illuminated by the electric lights of the shaft.

'Yes, Jack,' replied Harry, 'and I'm happy to see you. I have a proposition to make you...'

'I won't hear anything until you give me news of Nell!' cried Jack Ryan.

'Nell is well, Jack, and in fact so well that, in a month or six weeks I hope to...'

'You're going to marry her, Harry?'

'I don't know what you're talking about, Jack!'

'That's possible, Harry, but I know what I shall do!'

'And what will you do?'

'I shall marry her myself, if you don't marry her first!' retorted Jack, bursting out laughing. 'St Mungo protect me! But I like her, gentle Nell! A young and good creature who has never left the mine, she's the perfect wife for a miner! She is an orphan like I am an orphan, and if you really aren't thinking about her, and as long as she wants your old friend, Harry...!'

Harry looked gravely at Jack. He let him speak, without even trying to reply to him.

'I'm not making you jealous am I, Harry?' asked Jack Ryan in a more serious tone.

'No, Jack,' replied Harry calmly.

'Yet, if you don't make Nell your wife, you don't expect that she will stay a spinster?'

'I don't expect anything,' replied Harry.

A winding of the ladder had just then allowed the two friends to separate, one to descend, the other to climb up the shaft. But they did not take the opportunity to do so.

'Harry,' said Jack, 'do you think that I was speaking seriously about Nell just then?'

'No, Jack,' replied Harry.

'Well then, I'm going to now.'

'You, speak seriously?'

'My good Harry,' replied Jack, 'I am capable of giving some

good advice to a friend.'

'So give it then, Jack.'

'Well, here it is! You love Nell with all the love she deserves, Harry. Your father, old Simon, your mother, old Madge, love her as if she was their child. Now, you could well make a little effort so that she really becomes their daughter! Why don't you marry her?'

'For you to be going so far in your suggestions, Jack,' replied Harry, 'do you know Nell's feelings?'

'There is nobody who doesn't know them, not even you, Harry, and it's for that reason that you aren't jealous of me or anyone else. But here's the ladder that is going down, and...'

'Wait, Jack,' said Harry, holding back his friend, whose foot had already left the landing for the mobile rung.

'Well done, Harry!' cried Jack laughing, 'you're going to tear me apart!'

'Listen seriously, Jack,' replied Harry, 'for, I too, am speaking seriously.'

'I'm listening... until the next winding, but no longer!'

'Jack,' resumed Harry, 'I haven't concealed the fact that I love Nell. My deepest desire is to make her my wife...'

'That's good.'

'But I have a scruple of conscience in asking her to take an irrevocable decision as she is now.'

'What do you mean, Harry?'

'I mean, Jack, that Nell has never left the depths of the mine where she was born, no doubt. She knows about nothing, knows nothing of the outside world. She has everything to learn with her eyes, and perhaps also with her heart. Who knows what her thoughts will be, when new impressions are born in her! She still has nothing earthly about her, and it seems to me that it would be cheating her, before she has decided in full knowledge on the life of the mine over all other. Do you understand me, Jack?'

'Yes... vaguely... I understand above all that you want to

make me miss the next winding!'

'Jack,' replied Harry in a grave voice, 'you shall listen to what I have to say to you, if this equipment should no longer function, and when this landing should be gone from under our feet!'

'About time, Harry! That's how I like to be spoken to! We were saying then, that before marrying Nell, you are going to send her to a boarding-school in Auld Reekie?'

'No, Jack,' replied Harry. 'I know well enough myself how to educate the girl who should be my wife!'

'And she won't want anything more, Harry!'

'But, beforehand,' resumed Harry, 'as I have just told you, I want Nell to have a real knowledge of the outside world. A comparison, Jack: if you loved a blind girl, and if someone just said to you, "In one month she will be cured!" wouldn't you wait until she had been cured before marrying her?'

'Yes, well, yes!' replied Jack Ryan.

'Well, Jack, Nell is still blind, and before making her my wife, I want her to be sure that it's me, that it's the conditions of my life that she prefers and accepts. I want her eyes to be finally opened to the light of day!'

'Good, Harry, good, very good!' cried Jack Ryan. 'I understand you this time. And when is the operation to be...?'

'In a month, Jack,' replied Harry. 'Nell's eyes are gradually getting used to the brightness of our discs. It's a preparation. In a month I hope she will have seen the earth and its wonders, the sky and its splendours! She will know that Nature has given horizons more distant to the human gaze than those of the mine! She will see that the limits of the universe are infinite!'

But, while Harry was letting himself be carried away by his imagination, Jack Ryan, leaving the landing, had jumped on to the oscillating rung of the machine.

'Eh, Jack,' cried Harry, 'where are you?'

'Below you,' replied the cheerful comrade. 'While you are elevating yourself to the infinite, I'm descending into the abyss!'

'Bye, Jack!' replied Harry, himself hanging on to the mounting ladder. 'I recommend that you don't speak to anyone about what I've just told you!'

'Not to anyone!' cried Jack Ryan, 'but on one condition however...'

'What's that?'

'That I accompany the two of you on the first excursion that Nell makes to the surface of the globe!'

'Yes, Jack, I promise,' replied Harry.

A new propulsion of the equipment placed a further, more considerable interval between the two friends. Their voices only just reached each other, very faintly.

And yet, Harry could still hear Jack shout:

'And when Nell has seen the stars, the moon and the sun, do you know what she will prefer to them?'

'No, Jack!'

'You, my friend, still you, always you!'

And the voice of Jack Ryan finally petered out with a final hurrah.

Meanwhile, Harry dedicated all his unfilled hours to the education of Nell. He had taught her to read and to write – things in which the young girl made rapid progress. You would have said that she 'knew' by instinct. Never did sharp intelligence triumph more quickly over such complete ignorance. It was astonishing to those who were close to her.

Each day Simon and Madge felt more closely connected to their adoptive child, whose past nevertheless preoccupied them. They had well recognised Harry's feelings for Nell, and that did not displease them.

We remember during the engineer's first visit to the other cottage, the old overman had said to the engineer:

'Why would my son marry? What creature from up there would suit a lad whose life must be spent in the depths of a mine!'

Well, did it not seem as if Providence itself had sent the only companion who could truly suit his son? Was it not like a gift from Heaven?

Therefore, the old overman promised himself that if the marriage took place, that day, there would be a celebration in Coal City to go down in the history of the miners of New Aberfoyle.

Simon Ford could not have spoken a truer word.

It must be added that another desired this union no less ardently than Nell and Harry. It was the engineer James Starr. Certainly, he wanted above all the happiness of these two young people. But another motive, a more general interest, perhaps, also pushed him in that direction.

We know that James Starr retained certain apprehensions, although nothing any longer justified them. Nevertheless, what had been before could be again. Nell was clearly the only one to know the mystery of the new mine. But, if the future should hold new dangers for the Aberfoyle miners, how to guard against such eventualities, without at least knowing the cause?

'Nell has not wanted to talk,' repeated James Starr often, 'but what she has kept quiet about until now from all others, she will not know how to keep from her husband for long! The danger will threaten Harry like it will threaten us. So a marriage that gives happiness to the spouses and security to their friends, is a good marriage, or there will never be one down here!'

So reasoned the engineer James Starr, not without some logic. He even communicated this reasoning to old Simon, who found it to his taste. It seemed therefore that nothing should stand in the way of Harry becoming Nell's husband.

And indeed who could have done so? Harry and Nell loved each other. The old parents did not imagine another companion for their son. Harry's comrades envied his happiness, while recognising that he well deserved it. The young girl was dependent only on herself, and needed only the consent of her own heart.

But, if no one seemed to present an obstacle to this marriage, why, when the electrical discs went out at the hour of rest, when

Why would this enigmatic creature... come crawling...

night fell on the workers' city, when the inhabitants of Coal City had returned to their cottages, why, from one of the darkest corners of New Aberfoyle, would a mysterious being creep in the shadows? What instinct would guide this ghost across certain tunnels so narrow that one would think they were impenetrable? Why would this enigmatic creature, whose eyes pierced the darkest obscurity, come crawling on the banks of Loch Malcolm? Why would it head so obstinately towards Simon Ford's habitation, and so prudently too that it had until now thwarted all surveillance? Why would it come to press its ear to the windows and try to overhear snippets of conversation through the shutters of the cottage?

And, when certain words reached it, why would it raise its fist to threaten the peaceful residence? Why, finally did these words escape from a mouth contracted by anger:

'Her and him! Never!'

CHAPTER SEVENTEEN

A Sunrise

ONE MONTH LATER – it was the evening of the 20th of August – Simon Ford and Madge were giving their best wishes to four tourists who were preparing to leave the cottage.

James Starr, Harry and Jack Ryan were going to take Nell to a ground that her foot had never trodden, to the bright light that her eyes had never seen.

The excursion was to extend over two days. James Starr, in agreement with Harry, wanted the young girl to have seen everything that she had not been able to see in the dark mine by the end of these forty-eight hours outside – that is to say all the various aspects of the globe, as if a moving panorama of towns, plains, mountains, rivers, lochs, firths, and seas were to be paraded before her eyes.

Now, in this part of Scotland, between Edinburgh and Glasgow, it seemed that Nature had wanted precisely to bring together these terrestrial wonders, and as for the skies, they would be there as everywhere, with their changing clouds, their serene or veiled moon, their radiating sun, their teeming stars.

The proposed excursion had therefore been planned in a manner to satisfy the conditions of this programme.

Simon Ford and Madge would have been very happy to accompany Nell; but, as we know, they would not willingly leave their cottage, and in the end they could not agree to abandon their subterranean home even for one day.

James Starr was going along as an observer, as a philosopher, very curious, from a psychological point of view, to observe Nell's naive impressions – and perhaps even to discover something of the mysterious events which had surrounded her childhood.

Harry was wondering, not without some apprehension, if a girl other than the one he loved and had known till then, would reveal herself during this rapid initiation into the affairs of the outside world.

As for Jack Ryan, he was as happy as a lark flying in the first rays of the sun. He was hoping that his contagious cheer would spread to his travelling companions. It was a way of paying for his invitation.

Nell was pensive and seemed preoccupied.

James Starr had decided, rather sensibly, that the departure should take place in the evening. It was better that the girl should pass from the shadows of the night to the brightness of the day through an imperceptible gradation. This result would be obtained because from midnight to midday, she would experience the successive phases of shadow and light, which her sight could gradually get accustomed to.

On leaving the cottage, Nell took Harry's hand and said to him, 'Harry, is it really necessary that I abandon our mine, few days though it may be?'

'Yes, Nell,' replied the young man, 'it must be done! It must be done for your sake and mine!'

'Yet, Harry,' resumed Nell, 'since you rescued me, I am as happy as can be. You have taught me. Is that not enough? What am I going to do up there?'

Harry looked at her without answering. The thoughts that Nell expressed were almost his.

'My girl,' said James Starr then, 'I understand your hesitation, but it is right that you come with us. Those whom you love are coming with you, and they will bring you back. Whether you wish to continue living in the mine afterwards, like old Simon, Madge and Harry, is up to you! I do not doubt that it should be so, and I approve of it. But, at least you will be able to compare what you leave with what you are taking on, and act in complete freedom. Come now!'

'Come, my dear Nell,' said Harry.

'Harry, I am ready to follow you,' replied the girl.

At nine o'clock, the last train of the tunnel pulled Nell and her companions to the surface of the county. Twenty minutes later, it dropped them at the station where the little branch that served New Aberfoyle joined the railway from Dumbarton to Stirling.

The night was already dark. From the horizon to the zenith some thin vapours still passed in the upper reaches of the sky, under the pressure of a north-westerly breeze that cooled the atmosphere. The journey had been fine. The night ought to be as well.

Arriving in Stirling, Nell and her companions left the train and immediately went out of the station.

Before them, between the tall trees, lay a road that led to the banks of the Forth.

The girl's first physical impression was the pure air, which her lungs breathed in avidly.

'Breathe well, Nell,' said James Starr, 'breathe this air full of all the invigorating sensations of the countryside!'

'What is that great smoke running above our heads?' asked Nell.

'Those are clouds,' replied Harry, 'they are the half-condensed vapours which the west wind drives.'

'Ah!' said Nell, 'How I would like to feel myself carried in their silent whirl! And what are these sparkling dots that glitter through the gaps in the clouds?'

'Those are the stars that I told you about, Nell. So many suns, so many centres of worlds, perhaps resembling our own!'

The constellations drew themselves more clearly now on the blue-black of the firmament, which the wind was gradually purifying.

Nell looked at these thousands of shining stars that teemed above her head.

'But,' she said, 'if they are suns, how can my eyes support their brightness?'

'Those are the stars...'

'My girl,' replied James Starr, 'these are indeed suns, but suns that revolve at an enormous distance. The nearest of these thousands of stars, whose rays reach us, is the star of Lyra, Wega, which you see there almost at the zenith, and it is still fifty thousand billion leagues away, and no human eye can stare at it, for it is more fiery than the hearth of a furnace. But come, Nell, come!'

They took the road. James Starr was holding the girl by the hand. Harry was walking at her side. Jack Ryan was to-ing and fro-ing like a young dog, impatient at the slowness of his masters.

The path was deserted. Nell was watching the silhouette of the tall trees that the wind moved in the dark. She could have easily taken them for gesticulating giants. The rustling of the breeze in the high branches, the deep silence during the lulls, the line of horizon that become more clearly marked when the road cut a field, all impregnated her with new sensations and marked indelible impressions on her. After at first asking questions, Nell became quiet, and with a common purpose, her companions respected her silence. They did not want to influence the girl's sensitive imagination with their words. They preferred to let the ideas take root in her mind by themselves.

At around half past eleven, they reached the northern bank of the Firth of Forth.

There, a small boat that had been arranged by James Starr was waiting. In a few hours it should carry him and his companions to the port of Edinburgh.

Nell saw the shining water, which undulated at her feet with the action of the backwash and seemed studded with flickering stars.

'Is it a loch?' she asked.

'No,' replied Harry, 'it's a vast firth with flowing waters, it's the mouth of a river, it's almost a branch of the sea. Take a little of this water in the cup of your hand, Nell, and you will see that it isn't freshwater like Loch Malcolm.'

The young girl bent down, dipped her hand in the first waves and brought it to her lips.

'This water is salty,' she said.

'Yes,' replied Harry, 'the sea has flowed right up to here, because the tide is full. Three quarters of our globe is covered in this salt water, some drops of which you have just drunk!'

'But if the water of the rivers is just sea-water brought by the clouds, why is it fresh?' asked Nell.

'Because the water desalinates when it evaporates,' replied James Starr. 'The clouds are formed from only the evaporation and send this fresh water back to the sea in the form of rain.'

'Harry, Harry!' cried the young girl, 'what is this reddish glow that burns the horizon? Is it a forest on fire?'

And Nell pointed to a spot in the sky, among the low mists that were becoming coloured in the east.

'No, Nell,' replied Harry. 'It is the moon rising.'

'Yes, the moon!' cried Jack Ryan, 'a superb plate of silver which the celestial spirits make go round the firmament, and which gathers a whole mint of stars!'

'Really, Jack!' replied the engineer laughing, 'I did not know that you had this penchant for rash comparisons!'

'Ah! Mr Starr, my comparison is fair! Do you see that the stars are disappearing as the moon advances. I suppose then that they are falling inside!'

'In fact, Jack,' replied the engineer, 'it is the moon that is putting out the stars of the sixth magnitude with its brightness, and that is why they are disappearing in its passage.'

'How beautiful it all is!' repeated Nell, who was living only through her sight. 'But I thought that the moon was completely round?'

'It is round when it is full,' replied James Starr, 'that is to say when it finds itself in opposition to the sun. But tonight, the moon is entering its last quarter so it is already a crescent, and the silver plate of our friend Jack is nothing more than a shaving dish!'

'Ah! Mr Starr,' cried Jack Ryan, 'what an unworthy comparison! I was just about to strike up this couplet in honour of the moon:

Star of night which in your course
Comes to caress...

'But no! It's impossible now! Your shaving dish has destroyed my inspiration!'

Meanwhile, the moon was gradually mounting on the horizon. In front of it, the last mists disappeared. At the zenith and in the west, the stars still glittered on a black background that the moonlight would gradually whiten. Nell was contemplating this fine spectacle in silence; her eyes bore this soft silvery glimmer without tiring, but her hand shivered in Harry's, and spoke for her.

'Let's embark, my friends,' said James Starr. 'We have to climb Arthur's Seat before sunrise!'

The boat was moored at a post on the bank. A bargeman was guarding it. Nell and her companions boarded it. The sail was hoisted and was billowed by the north-west wind.

What a novel sensation the young girl felt then! She had navigated occasionally on the lochs of New Aberfoyle, but the oar, gently pulled by Harry as it was, always betrayed the effort of the rower. Here, for the first time, Nell felt herself carried along, gliding almost as smoothly as a balloon through the atmosphere. The firth was calm as a lake. Half lying at the back, Nell let herself be taken by the rocking. Occasionally, at certain movements, a moon ray would filter through to the surface of the Forth, and the craft seemed to sail on a sheet of shimmering silver. Little undulations babbled the length of the bank. It was a delight.

But it happened that Nell's eyes closed involuntarily. A sort of passing drowsiness overcame her. Her head leant on Harry's chest, and she fell into a peaceful sleep.

Harry wanted to wake her, so that she would not miss any of the magnificence of this beautiful night.

The firth was calm as a lake.

'Let her sleep, my boy,' said the engineer. 'Two hours of rest will better prepare her to bear the impressions of the day.'

At two o'clock in the morning, the craft reached Granton Pier. Nell woke up, as soon as it touched ground.

'Was I asleep?' she asked.

'No, my girl,' replied James Starr. 'You simply dreamed that you were asleep, that is all.'

The night was very clear now. The moon, at mid-path from the horizon to the zenith, spread its rays to all the corners of the sky. The little port of Granton contained just two or three fishing boats that rocked gently on the swell of the firth. The wind was falling with the approach of morning. The air, clear of mists, promised one of those delicious August days that proximity to the sea makes lovelier still. A sort of warm steam cleared from the horizon, but so fine, so transparent, that the first blazes of the sun would drink it in an instant. The girl could therefore observe the sight of the sea where it merges with the extreme perimeter of the sky. The range of her vision had increased, but her sight still did not experience that particular impression that the ocean gives, when the light seems to push back its bounds to infinity.

Harry took Nell's hand. The two of them followed James Starr and Jack Ryan, who were advancing through the deserted streets. In Nell's mind, this suburb of the capital was just a collection of dark houses which reminded her of Coal City, the sole difference being that its ceiling was higher and glittered with sparkling dots. She went with a light step, and Harry was never obliged to slow his own for fear of tiring her.

'Are you not weary?' he asked her, after half an hour of walking.

'No,' she replied. 'My feet don't seem to be touching the ground! This sky is so high above us that I have an urge to fly, as if I had wings!'

'Hold her back!' cried Jack Ryan. 'Because she's worth keeping, our little Nell! I experience this effect too, when I go for a time without leaving the mine.'

'It is due,' said James Starr, 'to the fact that we no longer feel cramped by the shale vault that covers Coal City. The firmament then seems like a deep abyss into which we are tempted to leap. Is that not what you feel, Nell?'

'Yes, Mr Starr,' replied the young girl, 'it is indeed that. I am experiencing a sort of vertigo!'

'You'll get used to it, Nell,' replied Harry. 'You'll get used to the immensity of the outside world, and perhaps then you will forget our dark mine!'

'Never, Harry!' replied Nell.

And she pressed her hand to her eyes, as if she wanted to restore to her mind the memory of all that she had just left.

Between the sleeping houses of the city, James Starr and his companions crossed Leith Walk. They walked round Calton Hill, where the Observatory and Nelson's Column stood in the half-darkness. They followed Regent Road, crossed a bridge, and arrived, by a slight detour, at the end of the Canongate.

There was not yet any movement in the city. The gothic clock of Canongate Kirk sounded three.

At this place, Nell stopped.

'What is that hazy mass?' she asked, pointing to an isolated edifice which rose at the bottom of a small square.

'That mass, Nell,' replied James Starr, 'is Holyrood, the palace of the former sovereigns of Scotland, where so many gloomy events have happened! There, the historian could evoke many a royal ghost, from the ghost of the unfortunate Mary Stuart to that of the old French King Charles x! And yet, despite these gloomy memories, when day comes, Nell, you will not find at this residence so lugubrious a sight! With its four great crenelated towers, Holyrood rather resembles some country-house, where the owner has conserved its feudal character for his own pleasure. But, let us continue our walk. There, in the very grounds of the former Holyrood Abbey, stand the superb Salisbury Crags, which are dominated by Arthur's Seat. That is

The castle, set on its basalt rock...

what we are going to climb. It is at its summit, Nell, that your eyes shall see the sun rise above the sea's horizon.'

They entered the Queen's Park. Then, gradually ascending, they crossed the Queen's Drive, a magnificent circular road passable by carriage, which Walter Scott claims to have obtained by writing a few lines in a novel.

Arthur's Seat is, in fact, only a hill of seven hundred and fifty feet, but its isolated head dominates the surrounding heights. In less than half an hour, by a winding path that makes the ascent easy, James Starr and his companions reached the head of the lion, which Arthur's Seat resembles when seen from the west side.

There, all four sat down, and James Starr, always ready with quotations of the great Scottish novelist, contented himself to say:

'Here's what Walter Scott wrote, in chapter eight of *The Heart of Midlothian*:

If I were to choose a spot from which the rising or setting sun could be seen to the greatest possible advantage, it would be that.

'So wait, Nell. The sun will not be long in appearing, and for the first time, you will be able to contemplate it in all its splendour.'

The girl's eyes were therefore turned towards the east. Harry, close to her, was watching her anxiously. Would she not be too strongly impressed by these first rays of daylight? All stayed silent. Even Jack Ryan was quiet.

Already a little pale line, nuanced in pink, was being drawn above the horizon on a background of light mist. A remnant of thin clouds, astray in the zenith, was attacked by the first stroke of light. At the foot of Arthur's Seat, in the absolute calm of the night a still drowsy Edinburgh hazily appeared. Some points of light pierced the darkness here and there. They were the morning stars that the people of the Old Town were lighting. Behind, in the west, the horizon, intersected by random silhouettes, marked the boundary of a region of hilly peaks, on which each sunray would place a feather of fire.

Meanwhile, the edge of the sea was becoming more clearly defined towards the east. The range of colours was gradually drawing up in the order of the solar spectrum. The red of the first mists was turning tone by tone to the violet of the zenith. With each second the palette became more intense: pink became red, red became fire. The day was forming at the point of intersection that the diurnal arc was about to make with the circumference of the sea.

At this moment, Nell's eyes were scanning from the foot of the hill to the city, where the different quarters were becoming distinguishable. Some pointed steeples emerged here and there on high monuments, and their outlines stood out more sharply. There spread a sort of ashen light. Finally, a first ray reached the girl's eye. It was the green ray, which in the evening or morning, escapes from the sea when the horizon is pure.

Half a minute later, Nell stood up and stretched her hand towards a point that dominated the area of the New Town.

'A fire!' she said.

'No, Nell,' replied Harry, 'it's not a fire. It's the golden touch of the sun on the top of the Scott Monument!'

And, indeed, the extreme tip of the pinnacle, two hundred feet high, was glowing like a superb lighthouse.

Day had come. The sun burst forth. Its disc still seemed damp, as if it had really risen from the waters of the sea. Initially stretched by refraction, it gradually shrunk to a circle. Its brightness, soon unbearable, was like the mouth of a furnace hollowed in the sky.

Nell immediately had to almost close her eyes. Over her too thin eyelids she still had to place her fingers, tightly closed.

Harry wanted her to turn towards the opposite horizon.

'No, Harry,' she said, 'my eyes have to get used to seeing what your eyes can see.'

Through the palm of her hands, Nell could still make out a pink glow, which whitened as the sun rose above the horizon. Her eyes gradually got used to it. Then, her eyelids opened, and her eyes finally beheld the light of day.

The pious child fell to her knees, crying:

'God, how beautiful your world is!'

The girl lowered her eyes then and looked. At her feet unfolded the panorama of Edinburgh: the new and carefully arranged areas of the New Town, the jumbled mass of houses and strange network of streets of the Old Town. Two heights dominated this ensemble: the castle, set on its basalt rock, and Calton Hill, with the modern ruins of a Greek monument on its rounded summit. Magnificent tree-lined roads radiated from the capital to the countryside. To the north, the Firth of Forth cut deeply into the coast, onto which opened the port of Leith. Above, in the distant background, lay the harmonious coast of the county of Fife. A road, straight as the road to Piraeus, linked this Athens of the North to the sea. Towards the west stretched the fine beaches of Newhaven and Portobello, whose sand tinted the first waves of the surf with yellow. In the open sea, some launches animated the waters of the firth, and two or three steamers plumed the sky with a cone of black smoke. Then, beyond, lay the vast green ocean. Modest hills dented the plain here and there. To the north, the Lomond Hills, in the west Ben Lomond and Ben Ledi reflected the solar rays, as if eternal ice had covered the peaks.

Nell could not speak. Her lips only murmured vague words. Her arms were shaking. Her head was spinning with vertigo. One moment and her strength failed her. In this air so pure, before this sublime spectacle, she felt suddenly weak, and fell unconscious into Harry's waiting arms.

This girl, whose life had until then been spent in the entrails of the terrestrial mass, had finally contemplated what almost the whole universe was made up of, such as the Creator and Man had made it. After having glided over the city and the countryside for the first time, her gaze just then stretched over the vastness of the sea and the infinity of the sky.

CHAPTER EIGHTEEN

From Loch Lomond to Loch Katrine

HARRY, CARRYING NELL in his arms, followed by James Starr and Jack Ryan, descended the slopes of Arthur's Seat. After several hours of rest and a fortifying breakfast at Lambret's Hotel, it was decided to complete the excursion with a trip through the lochs region.

Nell had recovered her strength. Her eyes were now able to open wide in the light, and her lungs to breathe deeply the invigorating and salubrious air. The green of the trees, the varied tones of the plants, the azure of the sky, had deployed the full range of colours before her eyes.

The train, which they caught at the General railway station, took Nell and her companions to Glasgow. From the last bridge over the Clyde, they were able to admire the curious maritime activity of the river. They spent the night at the Comrie's Royal Hotel.

The next day, from the Edinburgh and Glasgow railway station, the train took them quickly via Dumbarton to Balloch, at the southern extremity of Loch Lomond.

'This is the land of Rob Roy and Fergus MacGregor!' cried James Starr, 'the territory so poetically celebrated by Walter Scott! Do you not know this region, Jack?'

'I know it from its songs, Mr Starr,' replied Jack Ryan, 'and when a land has been sung about so well, it must be superb!'

'That it is, indeed,' cried the engineer, 'and our dear Nell will have the best memory of it!'

'With a guide such as yourself, Mr Starr,' replied Harry, 'it will be of double interest, for you will tell us the history of the land while we are looking at it.'

'Yes, Harry,' said the engineer, 'as far as my memory will

allow me to, but on one condition, however: that is that joyful Jack helps me! When I am tired of talking, he shall sing!'

'You won't have to ask me twice,' retorted Jack Ryan, sounding a vibrating note, as if he wanted his throat to rise to A in the scale.

It was just twenty miles by rail from Glasgow to Balloch, between the commercial metropolis of Scotland and the southernmost point of Loch Lomond.

The train passed through the royal borough and county town of Dumbarton, whose castle, still fortified in accordance with the treaty of the Union, is picturesquely set on the two peaks of a large basaltic rock.

Dumbarton is situated at the confluence of the Clyde and the Leven. A propos of this, James Starr recounted some details of the colourful history of Mary Stuart. For this was the borough that she left in order to go to marry Francis II and become Queen of France. Also, the British prime minister considered interning Napoleon there after 1815; but the choice of St Helena prevailed, which is why Britain's prisoner would die on a rock in the Atlantic, to the great advantage of his legend.

Soon, the train stopped at Balloch, near a wooden landing stage that descended to the level of the loch.

A steamboat, the *Sinclair*, was waiting for tourists wishing an excursion on the lochs. Nell and her companions embarked, after taking a ticket for Inversnaid, at the northernmost end of Loch Lomond.

The day began with a beautiful sun, free from those British mists, which normally veil it. No detail of this landscape, which would unfold over a journey of thirty miles, would escape the voyagers of the *Sinclair*. Nell, seated at the back between James Starr and Harry, was soaking up the superb poetry of the beautiful Scottish nature through all her senses.

Jack Ryan was walking to and fro on the *Sinclair*'s bridge, endlessly questioning the engineer, who did not, however, need to be asked. As the land of Rob Roy unfolded in front of their eyes, he would describe it as a keen admirer.

First numerous little isles or islets appeared close to the shores of Loch Lomond. It was as though they had been sown there. The *Sinclair* sidled round their steep banks, and in the midst of the isles, now a solitary valley stood out, now a wild gorge, bristling with steep rocks.

'Nell,' said James Starr, 'each of these islets has its legend, and perhaps its song, just like the hills that encircle the loch. One could say, without too much pretension, that the history of this land is written in the larger-than-life characters that are these isles and mountains.'

'Do you know, Mr Starr,' said Harry, 'what this part of Loch Lomond reminds me of?'

'What does it remind you of, Harry?'

'The thousand isles of Lake Ontario, so admirably described by Cooper. You must be struck by this resemblance as well, my dear Nell, for I read you his novel – which can justly be called the American author's finest – a few days ago.'

'Indeed, Harry,' replied the girl, 'it is the same sight, and the *Sinclair* is gliding between these isles just as Jasper Freshwater's cutter did on Lake Ontario.'

'Well,' resumed the engineer, 'that proves that the two sites equally merit being sung about by two poets! I do not know these thousand isles of Lake Ontario, Harry, but I doubt that their appearance could be more varied than this archipelago of Loch Lomond. Look at this landscape! There's Inchmurrin, with the old Lennox Castle, where the old Countess of Albany lived after the deaths of her father, husband and two sons, beheaded on the orders of James I. There's Clairinch, Creinch and Torrinch, some of which are rocky and wild with no trace of vegetation, while others have green and rounded hilltops. Here, larches and birches. There, fields of yellow and dried heather. In truth, I have difficulty in believing that the thousand isles of Lake Ontario offer such a variety of sites!'

'What is that little port?' asked Nell, who had turned

towards the eastern bank of the loch.

'It is Balmaha, which forms the entrance to the Highlands,' replied James Starr. 'The ruins that you see, Nell, are of an old nunnery, and these sparse tombs hold various members of the MacGregor clan, whose name is still famous throughout the land.'

'Famous for the blood that that clan has spilled and had spilled!' observed Harry.

'You are right,' replied James Starr, 'and it must be conceded that the fame won from battles is still the most long-lived. They last through the ages, tales of combat...'

'And they are perpetuated by songs,' added Jack Ryan.

And to back this up, the good lad burst into the first couplet of an old battle song, which recounts the exploits of Alexander MacGregor of Glen Strae, against Sir Humphry Colquhoun of Luss.

Nell listened, but from these battle stories, she gained only a feeling of sadness. Why had so much blood been spilled on these plains, which the girl found immense, and where no one should be short of space?

The banks of the loch, which were three to four miles long, narrowed together at the little port of Luss. Nell could see for a moment the old tower of its ancient castle. Then the *Sinclair* turned back to the north, and there before the tourists' eyes appeared Ben Lomond, which rose to nearly three thousand feet above the level of the loch.

'What a wonderful mountain!' cried Nell, 'The view from the top must be beautiful!'

'Yes, Nell,' replied James Starr. 'Look how the summit rises proudly from the bed of oak, birch and larch that covers the lower zone of the mountain. From there, one can see two thirds of our old Caledonia. It was here that the MacGregor clan resided, on the eastern part of the loch. Not far away, the quarrels of the Jacobites and the Hanoverians bloodied these desolate valleys once again. There, during fine nights, rose the pale moon that the old tales call 'the MacFarlane lantern.' There, the echoes still repeat the immortal names of Rob Roy and MacGregor-Campbell!'

Ben Lomond, the last peak of the Trossachs, truly merited being immortalised by the great Scottish writer. As James Starr observed, there were higher mountains, whose summits were covered in eternal snow, but there was perhaps no corner of the world more poetic.

'And,' he added, 'when I think that Ben Lomond belonged entirely to the Duke of Montrose! His Grace owned a mountain like a bourgeois in London owns the lawn in his garden!'

Meanwhile, the *Sinclair* arrived at the village of Tarbet, on the opposite bank of the loch, where it dropped off the passengers going to Inverary. Ben Lomond could be seen from here in all its glory. Its flanks, striped by the beds of torrents, shone like sheets of melting silver.

As the *Sinclair* passed alongside the base of the mountain, the land became steeper and steeper. There was the odd isolated tree here and there, a few weeping willows, fronds from which were once used for hanging people of modest means.

'To economise on hemp,' observed James Starr.

The loch, meanwhile, was narrowing as it extended towards the north. The lateral mountains closed it in more tightly. The steamboat passed alongside a few more islands and islets, Inveruglas Isle and Eilean Vow, where stood the vestiges of a fortress belonging to the MacFarlanes. Eventually the two banks joined, and the *Sinclair* stopped at the little resort of Inversnaid.

There, while their lunch was being prepared, Nell and her companions went to visit a waterfall near the landing-point that poured into the loch from a great height. It was as if it had been planted there as a decoration for the benefit of tourists. A shaky bridge spanned the tumultuous waters, in the midst of fine spray. From this place, the view embraced a great part of Loch Lomond, and the *Sinclair* seemed to be no more than a dot on its surface.

Loch Katrine

Lunch over, it was time to go to Loch Katrine. Several carriages bearing the Breadalbane coat of arms – the family that once supplied wood and water to the fugitive Rob Roy – were at the disposal of the travellers and offered them all the comforts that distinguish British coach-making.

Harry installed Nell on top, as was the fashion of the day. Her companions and he took their places next to her. A magnificent coachman in red livery gathered the reins of his four horses in his left hand, and the team began to climb up the flank of the mountain, passing next to the winding bed of the waterfall.

The road was very steep. As it rose, the shape of the surrounding summits seemed to change. The whole chain on the opposite bank of the loch and the peaks of Arroquhar seemed to grow magnificently, towering over the valley of Inveruglas. To the left peaked Ben Lomond, revealing the steep slopes of its northern flank.

The land between Loch Lomond and Loch Katrine was a wild sight. The valley began with narrow gorges which ended at Glen Aberfoyle. This name painfully reminded the young girl of the terror-filled pits, at the bottom of which she had spent her childhood. Therefore James Starr hastened to distract her with his tales.

The region lent itself to them, moreover. It was on the banks of the little Loch Ard that the main events of Rob Roy's life had taken place. There rose up the sinister limestone rocks, mingled with boulders, which the actions of time and the atmosphere had hardened like cement. Miserable huts, like dens – what are called 'boorachs' – lay among ruined sheepfolds. It was impossible to tell whether they were inhabited by human creatures or by wild beasts. Some young children, their hair bleached by the rigours of the climate, were watching the coaches pass with wide dumbfounded eyes.

'Here,' said James Starr, 'is what indeed can be more specifically called Rob Roy country. It was here that the excellent Bailie Nicol Jarvie, worthy son of his father the deacon, was seized by the Duke of Lennox's militia. It was in this very place that he got stuck, suspended by the seat of his trousers, fortunately made out of good Scottish cloth, and not the lighter market stuff from France! Not far from the streams of the Forth, which feed the torrents of Ben Lomond, you can still see the ford that the hero crossed to escape from the soldiers of the Duke of Montrose. Ah! If they had known the dark retreats of our mine, they would have been able to thwart all the searches! You see, my friends, we cannot take a step in this region without meeting these mementoes of the past that inspired Walter Scott when he paraphrased the call to arms of the MacGregor clan in magnificent verse!'

'All that is well said, Mr Starr,' rejoined Jack Ryan, 'but, if it's true that Nicol Jarvie stayed suspended by the seat of his trousers, what becomes of our proverb 'clever is he who can take the trousers from a Scotsman'?'

'Well, Jack, you are right,' replied James Starr laughing, 'and that proves quite simply that, on that day, our bailie was not dressed in the style of his ancestors!'

'He was wrong not to do so, Mr Starr!'

'I do not disagree, Jack!'

After having climbed the steep slopes of the waterfall, the coach team descended into a treeless, waterless valley, covered only by sparse heather. In certain places some heaps of stones rose in pyramids.

'Those are cairns,' said James Starr. 'In the past each passer-by had to add a stone, to honour the hero lying in these tombs. The Gaelic saying, 'I will add a stone to your cairn,' comes from this. If the sons had kept the faith of their fathers, these piles of stones would now be hills. In truth, in this region, everything contributes to developing the natural poetry innate to Highlanders' hearts. It is like that in all mountainous countries: the imagination is excited by these wonders – if the Greeks had lived in a country of plains, they would never have invented ancient mythology!'

'Those are cairns,' said James Starr.

During these and many other discussions, the carriage entered the gorges of a narrow valley which had been very conducive to the frolics of the brownies familiar to the great Meg Merillies. They passed the little Loch Arklet on the left, and a steeply sloping road appeared, which led to the inn of Stronachlachar on the bank of Loch Katrine.

There, at the pierhead of a light landing-stage, bobbed a little steamboat, which bore, naturally enough, the name of *Rob Roy*. The travellers immediately boarded: it was about to leave.

Loch Katrine is just ten miles long, with a width that never exceeds two miles. The first hills of the shore are still imbued with great character.

'Here is the loch,' cried James Starr, 'which is accurately compared to a long eel! It is claimed that it never freezes. I do not know about that, but what must not be forgotten is that it served as a theatre for the exploits of the *Lady of the Lake*. I am certain that if our friend Jack was to look closely, he would see the faint ghost of the beautiful Ellen Douglas still gliding under its surface!'

'Certainly, Mr Starr,' replied Jack Starr, 'and why wouldn't I see her? Why wouldn't this pretty lady be as visible on the waters of Loch Katrine as are the bogles of the mine on the waters of Loch Malcolm?'

Just then, the clear sounds of the bagpipes were heard at the back of the *Rob Roy*.

There, a Highlander in national costume was warming up on his bagpipes of three chanters, the largest of which sounded G, the second B, and the smallest an octave above the large one. As for the pipe, pierced with eight holes, it gave a scale of G major, with F natural.

The Highlander's refrain was a simple, gentle and innocent song. One could really believe that these national melodies were a natural mix of the breath of the wind, the murmurs of waters and the rustling of leaves. The shape of the refrain, which returned at regular intervals, was strange. Its phrasing consisted of three bars of double time, and a bar of triple time, finishing on the weaker time. In contrast to the songs of old, it was in a major key, and it could be written as follows, in the numerical language that gives not the notes, but the intervals of tones:

5 | 1.2 | 35 5 | 1.765 | 22.22
  | 1.2 | 35 5 | 1.765 | 11.11

Jack Ryan was now a truly happy man. He knew this song of the lochs of Scotland. So, while the Highlander accompanied him on his bagpipes, his melodic voice sang a hymn dedicated to the poetic legends of old Caledonia:

Still waters of my native land
Keep watch for ever more, O,
On all our legends sweet and grand,
O bonnie lochs of Scotland, O!

On your banks we find the trace
Of heroes great and battles won
By stalwarts of a noble race
Of which Sir Walter oft has sung!
Here's the tower where witches ever
Round their cooking pot did mingle;
There the open slopes of heather,
Where comes again the ghost of Fingal.

Here around the hours of midnight
Elfins strut their crazy paces,
And appear in eerie light
The Covenanters' sober faces!
At evening on the rocky strand,
One can surprise him as he leads her,
Waverley, who sought the hand
Of passionate Flora MacIvor.

Now comes the Lady of the Lake,
Hither on her palfrey borne
And Diana hears the silence break
To the call of Rob Roy's horn.
Where have we heard this sound before,
Fergus midst his gathered clans
Playing his great pibrochs of war
To raise an echo round the Highlands?

No matter that we sometimes roam,
Romantic lochs! These gushing streams,
These rugged rocks, still signal home
And thus they ever fill our dreams!
The visions all too soon disband
Return we beg, return to us.
To you our Caledonian land,
To you the very heart of us!

Still waters of my native land
Keep watch for evermore, O,
On all our legends sweet and grand,
O bonnie lochs of Scotland, O!

It was three o'clock in the afternoon. The less hilly western banks of Loch Katrine stood out then in the double frame of Ben A'an and Ben Venue. Already, half a mile away, the narrow basin was visible, at the bottom of which the *Rob Roy* would disembark the passengers going to Stirling by Callander.

Nell was worn out by the continual excitement of her senses. Each time a new subject of admiration came into her sight one sole phrase came from her lips: 'My Lord! My Lord!' She needed some hours of rest, if only to fix the memory of so many wonders more durably in her mind.

At that moment, Harry had taken her hand. He looked at the

young girl with emotion and said to her:

'Nell, my dear Nell, soon we shall be back in our dark domain. Will you not miss something of what you have seen during these few hours spent in broad daylight?'

'No, Harry,' replied the young girl. 'I shall remember, but it will be with happiness that I shall return with you into our much-beloved mine.'

'Nell,' asked Harry in a voice that was vainly trying to contain his emotion, 'do you want a sacred union to join us forever before God and before men? Do you wish me for your husband?'

'I do, Harry,' replied Nell, looking at him with her eyes so pure, 'I do, if you believe that I can be worthy enough for your life...'

Nell had not finished this sentence, in which Harry's entire future was contained, when an inexplicable phenomenon occurred.

The *Rob Roy*, although still half a mile from the bank, experienced a sudden impact. Its keel had just struck the bottom of the loch, and despite all its efforts, the engine could not pull it back.

And if this accident had occurred, it was because to its eastern orientation Loch Katrine had suddenly been almost emptied, as if a huge crack had opened up in its bed. In a few seconds, it had been drained, like a shore at the ebb of a equinoctial great tide. Nearly its entire contents had drained into the bowels of the earth.

'My friends,' James Starr had cried, as if the reason for this phenomenon was suddenly revealed to him, 'God save New Aberfoyle!'

CHAPTER NINETEEN

A Final Threat

THAT DAY, IN NEW ABERFOYLE, the works were operating as usual. From far off, blasts of dynamite could be heard, exploding the coal-bearing seam. Here, the blows of picks and crowbars breaking off the coal; there, the grating of drills making holes in the sandstone or shale faults. Long hollow sounds were made. The air sucked in by the machines gushed through the ventilation tunnels. The wooden doors slammed shut under these violent gusts. In the lower tunnels, the trains of mechanically driven wagons passed at a speed of fifteen miles per hour, and the automatic bells warned the workers to huddle up in the shelters. The cages mounted and descended without pause, pulled by the enormous spools of the machines installed at ground level. The discs, turned on full, brightly illuminated Coal City.

Mining was therefore being conducted with the greatest activity. The seam was being broken off into the wagons, which came in their hundreds to be emptied into the tubs at the bottom of the production shaft. While some of the miners were resting after the night shift, the day teams were at work, without wasting an hour.

Simon Ford and Madge, their dinner over, were installed in the yard of the cottage. The old overman was taking his usual siesta. He was smoking his pipe, stuffed with excellent French tobacco. When the married couple chatted, it was to talk about Nell, their boy, James Starr and this excursion to the surface of the earth. Where were they? What were they doing at this moment? How could they stay outside for so long without feeling nostalgia for the mine?

Just then, an extraordinary violent roaring was heard. It

seemed as though an enormous cataract was rushing into the mine.

Simon Ford and Madge sprang up.

Almost immediately the waters of Loch Malcolm swelled up. A high wave, unfurling like a Mascaret tidal bore, invaded the banks and crashed against the cottage wall.

Simon Ford, seizing Madge, had quickly led her to the first floor of the house.

At the same time, cries rose up from all over Coal City, threatened by this sudden inundation. Its inhabitants were seeking refuge up on the high shale rocks that formed the shore of the loch.

Terror was at its peak. Already some families of miners, half-panicked, were hurrying towards the tunnel to reach the upper levels. It was as if the sea had burst into the mine, the tunnels of which penetrate as far as the North Channel. The crypt, vast as it was, would have been entirely flooded. Not one of the inhabitants of New Aberfoyle would have escaped death.

But when the first fugitives reached the mouth of the tunnel, they found themselves in front of Simon Ford, who had immediately left the cottage.

'Stop, stop, my friends!' the old overman cried to them. 'If our city is to be deluged, the flood will run more quickly than you, and nobody will escape it! But the waters are no longer coming! All danger seems to have been avoided.'

'And what about our companions working at the coal-face?' cried some of the miners.

'There is nothing to fear for them,' replied Simon Ford. 'The work is being done at a level higher than the bed of the loch!'

The facts proved the old overman right. The flood had happened suddenly; but, spread over the lower floor of the vast mine, it had had no effect other than to raise the level of Loch Malcolm several feet. Coal City therefore was not jeopardised, and it could be hoped that the inundation, drained into the lowest, still unexploited, depths of the mine, had not claimed

Simon Ford, seizing Madge, had quickly led her...

any victim.

As for this flood, whether it was due to the overflow of an interior sheet of water through the cracks of the rock mass, or whether some water course from above ground had been forced by its collapsed bed to the deepest levels of the mine, Simon Ford and his companions could not say. As for thinking that the event was a mere accident, such as sometimes happened in collieries, there was nobody that did not have their doubts about that.

But, the same evening, the cause was known. The newspapers of the region published the story of this strange phenomenon, which had occurred in the setting of Loch Katrine. Nell, Harry, James Starr and Jack Ryan, who had returned in all haste to the cottage, confirmed the story, and learned, to their great relief, that the damage in New Aberfoyle was only material.

The bed of Loch Katrine had suddenly collapsed. Its waters had irrupted through a large fissure into the mine. In the loch favoured by the Scottish writer, there remained just enough water to wet the pretty feet of the Lady of the Lake – at least in this southern part. It was reduced to a pond of several acres where the bed lay below the collapsed section.

What repercussions this strange event had! It was the first time, without a doubt, that a lake had emptied itself in a few instants into the bowels of the earth. There remained nothing but to cross it out on the maps of the United Kingdom, until it might be refilled – by public subscription – having first filled the crack. Walter Scott would have died of despair – if he had still been of this world!

This accident was explicable, after all. Indeed, between the deep cavity and the bed of the loch, the layer of Secondary rocks was thinned to a slim layer, following a peculiarity of the geological disposition of the rocks.

But, if this collapse seemed to have a natural cause, James Starr, Simon and Harry Ford wondered whether it ought not to be attributed to malevolence. Their suspicions returned more

The bed of Loch Katrine had suddenly collapsed.

forcefully to their minds. The evil spirit – was it going to recommence its attempts against the exploiters of the rich mine?

Some days later, James Starr was discussing it with the old overman and his son at the cottage.

'Simon,' he said, 'in my opinion, although the event can easily be explained, I have a presentiment that it fits into the category of those things for which we are still searching the cause.'

'I agree, Mr James,' replied Simon Ford, 'but if you want my opinion, let's not divulge anything, and carry out our investigations ourselves.'

'Oh!' cried the engineer, 'I know the result already!'

'Eh! What will it be?'

'We will find the proof of malevolence, but not of the malefactor!'

'Yet he exists!' replied Simon Ford. 'Where does he hide? Could one single being, however perverse he may be, see through such an infernal idea as provoking the collapse of a loch? Really, I'll end up believing like Jack Ryan that it is some will o' the wisp of the mine, who begrudges us our invasion of its domain!'

It goes without saying that Nell, as far as possible, was kept outside of these discussions. She did not make this difficult for them. However, her attitude testified that she shared the preoccupations of her adoptive family. Her sad face bore the mark of the internal struggles that agitated her.

Be that as it may, it was decided that James Starr, Simon and Harry Ford would return to the very place of the collapse, and that they would try to discover its causes. They would tell no one of their project. To anyone who did not know the factual background which served as his base, the view of James Starr and his friends must have seemed absolutely outlandish.

Some days later, all three, on a small boat steered by Harry, came to examine the natural pillars that supported the part of the mass into which the bed of Loch Katrine had sunk.

This examination proved them right. The pillars had been

attacked by mine blasts. The blackened traces were still visible, for the waters had lowered in a succession of infiltrations, and it was possible to reach the base of the pillars.

The fall of a portion of the vault of the dome had been planned, then executed by a man's hand.

'There is no possible doubt,' said James Starr. 'And who knows what would have happened if, instead of this little loch, the collapse had opened passage to the waters of a sea!'

'Yes!' cried the old overman with a feeling of pride, 'it would take nothing less than a sea to drown our Aberfoyle! But, once again, what interest can some being have in the ruin of our operations?'

'It is incomprehensible,' replied James Starr. 'This is not a matter of a band of common criminals who roam the land from the den where they shelter to steal and pillage! In three years such misdeeds would have revealed their existence! Neither does it involve, as I previously thought, smugglers or money forgers, hiding their guilty industry in some still unknown nook of these vast caverns, and with an interest, therefore, in chasing us away. You do not make either counterfeit money or contraband in order to keep it! Yet it is clear that an implacable enemy has sworn the destruction of New Aberfoyle, and that an interest drives him to look for all possible means of assuaging the hate that he has vowed against us! Too weak, no doubt, to act openly, he prepares his traps in the dark, but the intelligence that he deploys in them makes him a formidable enemy. My friends, he knows all the secrets of our domain better than us, because for so long he has escaped all our searches! He is a man of the trade, a master among masters – that much is certain, Simon. What we have discovered about his way of working is the clear proof. Let us see, have you ever had some personal enemy, on whom your suspicions could rest? Think carefully. There are monomaniacs of hate that time does not cure. Go far back in your life, if necessary. All that is happening is the work of a kind of cold and patient madness, which requires that you dig up your most distant memories on the matter.'

Simon Ford did not reply. One could see that the honest overman, before explaining himself, was candidly questioning all his past. Finally, raising his head:

'No,' he said, 'before God, neither Madge nor I have ever wronged anybody. We don't believe that we could have an enemy, not one!'

'Oh!' cried the engineer, 'If only Nell would speak at last!'

'Mr Starr, and you too, father,' replied Harry, 'I beg you, let's keep the secret of our enquiry to ourselves! Don't question my poor Nell! I sense that she is already anxious and tormented. I am certain that her heart contains with great pain a secret that is suffocating her. If she is silent, it is either that she has nothing to say, or that she doesn't think that she should speak! We cannot doubt her affection for us, for us all! If she tells me later what she has until now kept silent about, you shall be informed at once.'

'So be it, Harry,' replied the engineer, 'and yet, if Nell does knows something, this silence really is inexplicable!'

And as Harry was about to protest, the engineer added, 'Be calm. We shall not say a word to the girl who should be your wife.'

'And who would be without further delay, if you wanted it, father!'

'My boy,' said Simon Ford, 'in one month to the day, your marriage shall take place. Will you take the place of Nell's father, Mr James?'

'Count on me, Simon,' replied the engineer.

James Starr and his two companions returned to the cottage. They did not say anything about the result of their exploration, and for everyone in the mine, the caving in of the vaults remained a case of simple accident. There was just one loch fewer in Scotland.

Nell had gradually resumed her habitual occupations. She had conserved undying memories from the visit to the surface of the county, which Harry made use of in his teaching. But this initiation to life outside had left her no regrets. She loved, as she had before the expedition, the dark domain where she would continue to reside as a women, having spent her childhood and adolescence there.

Meanwhile, the forthcoming marriage of Harry Ford and Nell had caused a great stir in New Aberfoyle. Congratulations flooded the cottage. Jack Ryan was not the last to bring his. He was to be discovered far away practising his best songs for a celebration in which the whole population of Coal City should take part.

But it happened that, during the month that preceded the marriage, New Aberfoyle was more afflicted than it had ever been before. It might be said that the approach of the union of Nell and Harry was causing disaster after disaster. The accidents occurred principally at the coal-face, without the true cause being discernable.

Thus, a fire devoured the timberwork of a lower gallery, and the lamp that the arsonist had used was found. Harry and his companions had to risk their lives to put out this fire, which threatened to destroy the seam, and they only managed it by using extinguishers filled with a solution of carbonic acid, with which the colliery was prudently supplied.

Another time, it was a caving in due to the rupture of the props of a shaft, and James Starr noted that these props had been attacked with a saw beforehand. Harry, who was surveying the works at this place, was buried under the rubble and only escaped death by a miracle.

Some days later, on the mechanical tramway, the train of wagons on which Harry was mounted, crashed into an object and was overturned. Later it was seen that a beam had been placed across the rails.

In short, these events multiplied to such an extent that a sort of panic broke out among the miners. It required nothing less than the presence of their bosses to keep them at their work.

Harry was buried under the rubble...

'But there are a whole band of them, these criminals!' repeated Simon Ford, 'and we cannot put our hands on a single one!'

The searches were resumed. The county police were on their feet day and night, but they could find nothing. James Starr forbade Harry, to whom this malevolence seemed most directly aimed, ever to venture away from the centre of the works alone.

They behaved all the same with consideration for Nell, from whom, on Harry's insistence, they concealed all these criminal attempts, which might bring back to her an old memory of the past. Simon Ford and Madge watched her day and night with a sort of severity, or rather, a fierce anxiety. The poor child realised it; but not a remark, not a complaint escaped her. Did she say to herself that if they were acting so, it was in her interest? Yes, probably. However, she too, in her way, seemed to watch over the others, and only appeared calm when all those she loved were together in the cottage. In the evening, when Harry returned, she could not contain a movement of mad joy, out of character with her ordinarily more reserved than expansive nature. Once night passed, she was up before all the others. Her anxiety resumed from the morning at the hour of the departure for the coal-face.

In order to give her some respite, Harry had wanted their marriage to have already taken place. It seemed to him that faced with this irrevocable act, the malevolence, rendered useless, would abate, and that Nell would not feel secure until she was his wife. This impatience was moreover shared by James Starr, as well as by Simon Ford and Madge. Each was counting the days.

The truth is that they were each in the grip of the most sinister forebodings. This hidden enemy, that they knew not where to catch nor how to fight, was without doubt, it was whispered, indifferent to nothing where Nell was concerned. The solemn act of the marriage of Harry and the girl could therefore be the occasion of some new machination of its hate.

One morning, eight days before the time set for the ceremony, Nell, pushed no doubt by some sinister presentiment, managed to be the first to leave the cottage, the surroundings of which she wanted to observe.

Her cry resounded in the whole habitation, and instantly brought Madge, Simon and Harry to the girl.

Nell was as pale as death, her face distraught, betraying an inexpressible horror. Unable to speak, her eyes were fixed on the cottage door, which she had just opened. Her tense hand was pointing to these lines on it, which had been marked during the night, the sight of which terrified her:

Simon Ford, you have stolen the last seam of our old mines from me! Harry, your son, has stolen Nell from me! Woe betide you! Woe betide you all! Woe betide New Aberfoyle!

Silfax

'Silfax!' cried Simon Ford and Madge in unison.

'Who is this man?' asked Harry, who looked alternately at his father and the girl.

'Silfax!' repeated Nell with despair, 'Silfax!'

And her whole body trembled in murmuring this name, while Madge seized her and led her almost by force to her room.

James Starr had rushed up. After having read and reread the menacing phrases, he said:

'The hand that wrote these lines is the one that had written me the letter contradicting yours, Simon! This man is called Silfax. I see by your turmoil that you know him. Who is this Silfax?'

Simon Ford, you have stolen the last seam from me.

CHAPTER TWENTY

The Penitent

THIS NAME HAD been a total revelation for the old overman.

It was the name of Dochart Pit's last penitent.

In the past, before the introduction of the safety lamp, Simon Ford had known this staunch man who would risk his life in going each day to provoke the partial explosions of the firedamp. He had seen this strange being prowling in the mine, always accompanied by an enormous snowy owl, a monstrous sort of bird, which helped him in his perilous occupation by carrying a lit wick to where Silfax's hand could not reach. One day, this old man had disappeared, along with a little orphan girl, born in the mine, and who had no other relative except him, her great-grandfather. This child was evidently Nell. For fifteen years the two of them had therefore lived in some secret retreat, until the day Nell was saved by Harry.

The old overman, beset with both pity and anger, conveyed to the engineer and to his son what the sight of the name of Silfax had just revealed to him.

This illuminated the whole situation. Silfax was the mysterious being vainly sought in the depths of New Aberfoyle.

'So, you knew him, Simon?' asked the engineer.

'Yes, indeed,' replied the overman. 'The man with the owl! He was already old. He must have been fifteen or twenty years older than me. A sort of wild man, who mixed with nobody, who seemed to fear neither water nor fire! He had deliberately chosen the job of penitent, which few cared for. This dangerous profession had deranged his thoughts. He was said to be evil – he was perhaps just mad. His strength was prodigious. He knew the mine like no other – at the least as well as me. He was given some sort of allowance. Heavens, I thought him dead years ago.'

'But,' resumed James Starr, 'what does he mean by the words, "You have stolen the last seam of our old mines from me"?'

'Ah, yes,' replied Simon Ford, 'For a long time already, Silfax, whose mind, as I have said, had always been deranged, claimed to have rights over old Aberfoyle. So his temper become increasingly bitter as Dochart Pit – his pit – became exhausted. It seemed that each strike of the pick was hacking his own entrails from his body! You must remember that, Madge?'

'Yes, Simon,' replied the old Scotswoman.

'It's coming back to me now,' resumed Simon Ford, 'since I saw the name of Silfax on the door; but I repeat, I thought he was dead, and I couldn't imagine that this criminal that we have searched for so much was the old penitent of Dochart Pit!'

'Indeed,' said James Starr, 'everything is explained. Chance revealed the existence of the new seam to Silfax. In his madman's egoism, he must have wanted to become its defender. Living in the mine, roaming it night and day, he would have discovered your secret, Simon, and known that you would ask me to come in all haste to the cottage. Hence this letter contradicting yours; hence, after my arrival, the block of stone thrown at Harry and the destroyed ladders of the Yarrow Shaft; hence, the sealing of the cracks in the wall of the new seam; hence, finally, our imprisonment, then our deliverance, which was achieved no doubt thanks to the benevolent Nell, without the knowledge of and despite this Silfax!'

'It must have occurred just as you have described, Mr James,' replied Simon Ford. 'The old penitent is definitely mad now!'

'That's just as well,' said Madge.

'I am not so sure,' resumed James Starr shaking his head, 'for his madness must be terrible! Ah, I understand why Nell could not think of him without terror, and I also understand why she would not want to denounce her grandfather. What sad years she must have spent with that old man!'

'Very sad,' replied Simon Ford, 'with this savage and his owl, no less savage than he! For, of course, this bird is not dead. It could only be it that put out our light and only it that wanted to cut the rope from which Harry and Nell were suspended!'

'And I understand,' said Madge, 'that the news of the marriage of his granddaughter to our son seems to have aggravated the rancour and redoubled the rage of Silfax!'

'Nell's marriage to the son of the man whom he accuses of having stolen the last seam of Aberfoyle from him, could only, indeed have brought his outrage to a peak!' continued Simon Ford.

'He ought nevertheless to play his part in our union!' cried Harry. 'However much a stranger to normal life, we'll surely end up bringing him to recognise that Nell's new life is worth more than the one he made for her in the abysses of the mine! I am sure, Mr Starr, that if we could put our hands on him, we would manage to make him see reason.'

'You cannot reason with insanity, my poor Harry!' replied the engineer. 'Better, without a doubt, to know one's enemy than not to know him; all is not lost, for we know today who he is. Let us stay on our guard, my friends, and to start with, Harry, Nell must be questioned. She must be! She will understand that her silence no longer has a purpose. In the interest even of her grandfather, it is appropriate that she speak. It is important, as much for him as for us, that we put an end to his sinister designs.'

'I do not doubt, Mr Starr,' replied Harry, 'that Nell will come of her own accord to face your questions. You know now that it was through conscience, through duty, that she has kept silent until now. It is through duty and conscience that she will speak as soon as you wish. My mother was right to take her to her room. She had great need of collecting her thoughts, but I will go and fetch her...'

'No need, Harry,' said the firm and clear voice of the girl, who was entering the large living room of the cottage at that very moment.

Nell was pale. Her eyes betrayed how much she had cried; but the others sensed her resolve in the step that her loyalty required of her at this time.

'Nell!' cried Harry, dashing towards the young girl.

'Harry,' replied Nell, who stopped her betrothed with a gesture, 'your father, your mother, and you – you must know everything today. You must not stay in the dark either, Mr Starr, about what concerns the child that you have welcomed without knowing her, and that Harry, to his misfortune, alas, pulled from the abyss.'

'Nell!' cried Harry.

'Let Nell speak,' said James Starr, imposing silence on Harry.

'I am the granddaughter of old Silfax,' resumed Nell. 'I never knew a mother until the day I came here,' she added, looking at Madge.

'Bless that day, my girl!' replied the old Scotswoman.

'I didn't know a father until the day I saw Simon Ford,' resumed Nell, 'and a friend until the day Harry's hand touched mine! I lived alone for fifteen years, in the most out of the way corners of the mine, with my grandfather. With him – that's going a bit far. By him would be more accurate. I hardly saw him. When he disappeared into old Aberfoyle, he took refuge in recesses that he alone knew. In his way, he was good to me then, however terrifying. He fed me with what he would go and search for outside; but I had the vague memory that, first, during my youngest years, I had a goat for a nurse, whose loss upset me greatly. Grandfather, seeing me grieve so, initially replaced it with another animal – a dog he told me. Unfortunately this dog was lively. It would bark. Grandfather didn't like liveliness. He had a horror of noise. He had taught me silence, but hadn't been able to teach it to the dog. The poor animal disappeared almost immediately. Grandfather had a snowy owl as a companion, which initially filled me with horror; but this bird, despite the repulsion it inspired in me, held such an affection for me that I ended up reciprocating it. It came to obey me better than its master, and even that worried me for its sake. Grandfather was jealous. The owl and I, we hid as far as we could the fact that we got on well together! We understood what we had to do... But that's to tell you too much about me! It's about you...'

'No, my girl,' replied James Starr. 'Tell things as they come to you.'

'My grandfather,' resumed Nell, 'had always seen your residence in the mine in a very bad light. There was no lack of space, however. It was far, very far from you that he chose his hideouts. But it displeased him to sense you there. When I questioned him about the people from up there, his face would darken, he wouldn't reply and would be silent for a long time. But his anger exploded when he perceived that, no longer content with the old domain, you seemed to want to encroach upon his. He swore that if you managed to penetrate the new mine, until then known to him alone, you would die! Despite his age, his strength is still extraordinary, and his threats made me tremble for you and for him.'

'Continue, Nell,' said Simon Ford to the girl, who had stopped a moment, better to recollect her memories.

'After your first attempt,' resumed Nell, 'as soon as Grandfather saw you enter the tunnel of New Aberfoyle, he blocked the opening and made a prison of it for you. I knew you only as shadows, vaguely seen in the dark mine; but I couldn't bear the idea that Christian people were going to die of starvation in these depths, and, at the risk of being caught red-handed, I managed for some days to procure for you a little bread and water... I would have wanted to guide you outside, but it was difficult to escape the surveillance of my grandfather. You were about to die! Jack Ryan and his companions arrived... God allowed me to meet them on that day! I led them to you. On the way back, my grandfather discovered me. His anger against me was terrible. I thought he was going to kill me! Since then, life became unbearable for me. My grandfather's ideas became

completely deranged. He proclaimed himself the king of darkness and fire! When he heard your picks hitting these seams that
he considered his own, he became furious and beat me with
rage. I wanted to escape. It was impossible, so closely did he
guard me. Finally, three months ago, in a fit of indescribable
insanity, he put me down the abyss where you found me, and he
disappeared, after having vainly summoned the owl, which
faithfully stayed with me. For how long was I there? I don't
know! All I know is that I thought that I was going to die, when
you arrived, Harry, and you saved me! But, you see, the granddaughter of Silfax cannot be the wife of Harry Ford, because he
will want your life, all your lives!'

'Nell!' cried Harry.

'No,' continued the girl. 'My sacrifice is made. There is only
one way to avert your death: that I return to my grandfather. He
is threatening all of New Aberfoyle! His heart is incapable of
forgiveness, and no one can know what the genius of vengeance
could inspire in him! My duty is clear. I would be the most
wretched of creatures if I hesitated to fulfil it. Farewell! And
thank you! You have made me know the happiness of this
world! Whatever happens to me, know that my whole heart will
rest amongst you!'

At these words, Simon Ford, Madge and Harry, mad with
grief, rose.

'What, Nell!' they cried with despair, 'You would like to
leave us!'

James Starr dismissed them with an authoritative gesture,
and going straight to Nell, he took her two hands.

'That is well said, my child,' he said to her. 'You have said
what you had to say; but here is what we have to say in reply.
We will not let you leave, and, if necessary, we shall hold you
back by force. Do you think us capable of the cowardice of
accepting your generous offer? However, you can, in the interest of Silfax himself, inform us about his habits, tell us where he
hides. We only want one thing: to render him harmless, and

perhaps to bring him back to reason.'

'You want the impossible,' replied Nell. 'My grandfather is everywhere and nowhere. I never knew his hideouts! I have never seen him sleep. When he had found some refuge, he would leave me alone and disappear. When I made up my mind, Mr Starr, I knew all that you would say in response. Believe me! There is only one way to disarm my grandfather: that is that I manage to find him. He himself is invisible, but he sees everything. Ask yourselves how he could have discovered your most secret thoughts, from the letter written to Mr Starr to the plan of my marriage with Harry, if he didn't have some inexplicable ability to know everything. My grandfather, as far as I can tell, even in his madness, is a man of powerful mind. In the past, he did sometimes tell me about great things. He taught me about God, and only tricked me on one point: that is when he made me believe that all men were treacherous, as he wanted to inspire in me his loathing for all humanity. When Harry brought me to this cottage, you thought that I was only ignorant! I was more than that. I was terrified! Oh, forgive me, but for several days I thought myself to be in the power of wicked people, and I wanted to flee you! The person who began to bring my mind back to the truth was you, Madge, not through your words, but by the vision of your life, when I saw how you were loved and respected by your husband and your son! Then, when I saw these happy and good workers, whom I initially thought were slaves, venerate Mr Starr, when for the first time I saw the whole population of New Aberfoyle come to the chapel, bend down on their knees, pray to God and thank him for his infinite bounty, then I said to myself, 'My grandfather has tricked me!' But today, enlightened by all that you have taught me, I think that he has tricked himself! I am therefore going to go back along the secret paths by which I accompanied him in the past. He must be watching me! I will call him... he will hear me, and who knows if, in returning to him, I won't make him see the light?'

Everyone had let the girl speak. Each sensed that it must have been good for her to open her heart completely to her friends, at the moment when in her generous illusion, she believed that she was about to leave them forever. But when, exhausted, her eyes brimming with tears, she was silent, Harry turned towards Madge and said:

'Mother, what would you think of a man who abandoned the noble girl that you have just listened to?'

'I would think,' replied Madge, 'that this man was a coward, and if he was my son, I would disown him, I would curse him!'

'Nell, you have heard our mother,' resumed Harry. 'Wherever you go, I will follow you. If you persist in leaving, we will leave together...'

'Harry, Harry,' cried Nell.

But the emotion was too much. The girl's lips went pale, and she fell into the arms of Madge, who asked the engineer, Simon, and Harry to let her be alone with her.

'Wherever you go, I will follow you,' said Harry.

CHAPTER TWENTY-ONE

Nell's Marriage

THEY WENT THEIR separate ways, but it was first agreed that the residents of the cottage would be on their guard more than ever. The threat of old Silfax was too direct for it not to be taken seriously. It was to be wondered whether the old penitent did not hold some terrible capability to annihilate all of New Aberfoyle.

Armed guards were therefore posted at the various openings of the mine, with orders to watch over them day and night. Every stranger to the mine had to be brought in front of James Starr, so that he could check his identity. They did not shrink from making the inhabitants of Coal City aware of the threats to which the subterranean colony was subject. As Silfax had no accomplice in the place, there was no fear of betrayal. Nell was informed of all the security measures that had just been put in place, and without being completely reassured, she found some peace of mind. But Harry's resolution to follow her wherever she went had more than anything else contributed to the extraction of her promise not to flee.

During the week that preceded Nell and Harry's marriage, no incident troubled New Aberfoyle. So the miners, without letting up the surveillance put in place, recovered from the panic that could have compromised the exploitation.

Meanwhile James Starr continued to have searches made for old Silfax. As the vindictive old man had declared that Nell would never marry Harry, it had to be conceded that he would shrink from nothing to prevent this marriage. Ideally, they would take him alive. The exploration of New Aberfoyle was therefore meticulously resumed. The tunnels were scoured as far as the higher levels that cropped out at the Dundonald Castle ruins in Irvine. It was rightly believed that it was through the old castle that Silfax communicated with the outside and stocked up on the items necessary for his miserable existence, either by buying or by thieving. As for the fire-maidens, James Starr had the thought that some jet of firedamp, which occurred in this part of the mine, could have been lit by Silfax and produced this phenomenon. He was not mistaken. But the searches were in vain.

During this continual struggle against an elusive creature, James Starr was, without letting it be seen, the most unhappy of men. As the day of the wedding approached, his fears increased, and he though that he should, exceptionally, confide in the old overman, who soon became more anxious than him.

Finally the day arrived.

Silfax had not given any sign of life.

As soon as it was the morning, the whole population of Coal City was on its feet. The New Aberfoyle works had been suspended. Supervisors and workmen were going to pay their respects to the old overman and his son. It was simply paying a debt of recognition to the two bold and persevering men, who had restored the mine to its former prosperity.

It was at eleven o'clock, in St Giles' Chapel, elevated on the bank of Loch Malcolm, that the ceremony was to take place.

At the appointed hour, Harry was seen leaving the cottage, giving his arm to his mother, while Simon Ford gave his arm to Nell.

There followed the engineer James Starr, impassive in appearance, but inside expecting anything, and Jack Ryan, superb in his piper's costume.

Then came the other engineers of the mine, the notables of Coal City, the friends, the companions of the old overman, all the members of this great family that made up the unique population of New Aberfoyle.

Outside, it was one of those torrid days of the month of August, which are particularly unpleasant in the countries of the north. The stormy air penetrated to the depths of the mine,

Armed guards were posted at the various openings.

where the temperature had risen abnormally. The atmosphere was saturated with static electricity through the ventilation shafts and the vast Malcolm tunnel.

One could have noted – quite a rare phenomenon – that the barometer in Coal City had fallen by a considerable amount. One might have wondered whether a storm was not going to burst under the shale vault that formed the sky of this immense crypt.

But the truth was that nobody inside was preoccupied with the atmospheric menaces outside.

Each person, it goes without saying, was dressed up in their finest clothes for the occasion.

Madge was wearing an outfit that resembled those of olden times. On her head she had a 'toy' headdress, like the old matrons, and on her shoulders was draped a 'rokelay', a sort of tartan mantle that Scotswomen wear rather elegantly.

Nell had promised herself to let none of the turbulences of her mind be visible. She forbade her heart to pound, her secret anguish to betray itself, and the courageous child managed to show everyone a calm and collected face.

She was simply presented, and the simplicity of her clothing, which she had preferred to more fancy trappings, added further charm to her person. Her only headdress was a 'snood', a multi-coloured band, which young Caledonian girls often wear.

Simon Ford's clothes would not have been disowned by Walter Scott's dignified Bailie Nicol Jarvie.

Everyone headed towards St Giles' Chapel which had been lavishly decorated.

In the sky of Coal City, the electric discs, brightened by an increase in current, dazzled like as many suns. An illuminated atmosphere filled the whole of New Aberfoyle.

In the chapel, electric lamps also projected bright glows, and the stained-glass windows shone like kaleidoscopes of fire.

The Reverend William Hobson was to officiate. He was awaiting the arrival of the betrothed right at the door of St Giles.

The procession approached, after majestically circling round the banks of Loch Malcolm.

At this moment the organ sounded, and the two couples, preceded by the Reverend Hobson, headed towards the chevet of St Giles.

The heavenly blessing was first called upon the whole congregation; then, Harry and Nell remained alone in front of the minister, who was holding the Holy Book in his hand.

'Harry,' asked the Reverend Hobson, 'do you take Nell to be your wife, and do you promise to love her always?'

'I do,' replied the young man in a strong voice.

'And you, Nell,' resumed the minister, 'Do you take as husband Harry Ford, and...'

The girl had not had the time to respond when an immense clamour resounded outside.

One of the enormous rocks, forming a terrace, overhanging the bank of Loch Malcolm, at a hundred paces from the chapel, had suddenly given way, without explosion, as if its fall had been prepared in advance. Below, the waters plunged into a deep hollow, that no one knew existed there.

Then suddenly, between the crumbled rocks, appeared a boat, which a vigorous thrust launched to the surface of the loch.

On this boat, an old man was standing upright, dressed in a dark cowl, his hair bristling, and a long white beard falling on his chest.

He had a Davy lamp in his hand, in which a flame was burning, protected by the metal grill of that apparatus.

At the same time, in a loud voice, the old man cried:

'The firedamp! The firedamp! Woe betide you all! Woe betide you!'

Just then, the light odour that characterises carburetted hydrogen gas spread in the atmosphere.

And if it was so, it was because the fall of the rock had given passage to an enormous quantity of the explosive gas, stored up in enormous 'blowers', the mouths of which had been blocked by the shale. The jets of firedamp seeped towards the vaults of the dome, under a pressure of five to six atmospheres.

The old man knew of the existence of these blowers, and had suddenly released them, so as to render the crypt's atmosphere explosive.

James Starr and some others, quickly left the chapel and hurried towards the bank.

'Out of the mine! Out of the mine!' cried the engineer, who, having understood the imminence of the danger, had just given this cry of alarm at the doors of St Giles.

'The firedamp! The firedamp!' repeated the old man, pushing his boat further forward on the loch's waters.

Harry, leading his betrothed, his father and his mother, had hurriedly left the chapel.

'Out of the mine! Out of the mine!' repeated James Starr.

It was too late to flee. Old Silfax was there, ready to accomplish his last threat, ready to prevent the marriage of Nell and Harry, by burying the entire population of Coal City under the ruins of the mine.

Above his head flew his enormous snowy owl, whose white plumage was dirty with black marks.

But then, a man rushed into the waters of the loch, and swam vigorously towards the boat.

It was Jack Ryan. He was striving to reach the madman before he could accomplish his act of destruction.

Silfax saw him coming. He broke the glass of his lamp, ripped out the lit wick and he waved it in the air.

A deadly silence spread through all the congregation on dry ground. James Starr, resigned, was amazed that the inevitable explosion had not already annihilated New Aberfoyle.

Silfax, his features tense, realised that the firedamp, too light to remain in the low layers, had accumulated in the heights of the dome.

But then the owl, at Silfax's gesture, seized the burning wick in its talon, as it had done in the past in the tunnels of Dochart Pit, and began to climb towards the high vault that the old man was pointing to.

A few seconds more, and New Aberfoyle's life would be over!

At that moment, Nell broke free from Harry's arms.

Calm and inspired at the same time, she ran towards the bank of the loch, as far as the water's edge.

'Owl! Owl!' she cried in a clear voice, 'To me! Come to me!!'

The faithful bird, surprised, had hesitated an instant. But then, having recognised Nell's voice, it let the burning wick fall to the waters of the loch, and tracing a large circle, swooped down to the girl's feet.

The explosive upper layers in which the firedamp had mixed with the air had not been lit.

Then a terrible cry resounded under the dome. It was the last that the old man gave.

Just when Jack Ryan was about to put his hand on the edge of the boat, the old man, seeing his vengeance escape him, thrust himself into the waters of the loch.

'Save him! Save him!' cried Nell in a harrowing voice.

Harry heard it. Leaping in his turn to swim, he had soon joined Jack Ryan and dived several times. But their efforts were useless.

The waters of Loch Malcolm did not surrender their prey. They were closed around old Silfax for good.

On a boat, old Silfax, his hair bristling...

CHAPTER TWENTY-TWO

The Legend of Old Silfax

SIX MONTHS AFTER these events, the marriage of Harry Ford and Nell, so strangely interrupted, was celebrated in St Giles' Chapel. After the Reverend Hobson had blessed their union, the young spouses, still dressed in mourning, returned to the cottage.

James Starr and Simon Ford, from then on free from all worry, presided joyously over the celebration which followed the ceremony and lasted until the following day.

It was in these memorable circumstances that Jack Ryan, dressed in his piper's costume, after having inflated the skin of his bagpipes, managed the triple achievement of playing, singing and dancing all at the same time, to the applause of everyone assembled.

And, the following day, the surface and pit-face works resumed, under the direction of the engineer James Starr.

Harry and Nell were happy – one hardly need say. These two hearts, so tested, found in their union the happiness that they deserved.

As for Simon Ford, the honorary overman of New Aberfoyle, he counted on living well enough to celebrate fifty years with the good Madge, who asked for nothing more.

'And after that, why not another?' said Jack Ryan. 'Two fifties, that wouldn't be too much for you, Mr Simon!'

'You are right, my lad,' replied the old overman calmly. 'What would be surprising if, in this climate of New Aberfoyle, in this environment that doesn't experience the extremes of weather outside, one lived to twice a hundred?'

Would the inhabitants of Coal City ever be present at this second ceremony? The future would tell.

In any case, a bird that seemed to have reached an extraordinary longevity was old Silfax's owl. It still haunted the dark domain. But with the death of the old man, although Nell had tried to keep it, it fled after a few days. Not only did the company of men decidedly no more please it that its old master, it seemed that it bore a particular rancour towards Harry, and that this jealous bird had always recognised and detested him as the first ravisher of Nell, he with whom it had fought in vain at the ascension of the chasm.

Since that time, Nell saw it again only at long intervals, gliding above Loch Malcolm.

Did it want to see its friend of yore again? Did it want to plunge its penetrating looks down to the bottom of the gulf that had swallowed up Silfax?

The two versions were accepted, for the owl became legendary, and it inspired in Jack Ryan more than one fantastical tale.

It is thanks to this cheerful companion that in Scottish evening gatherings songs are still sung of the legend of the bird of old Silfax, the former penitent of the Aberfoyle mines.

Some other books published by **LUATH** PRESS

Red Sky at Night
John Barrington
ISBN 0 946487 60 X PB £8.99

John Barrington is a shepherd to over 750 Blackface ewes who graze 2,000 acres of some of Britain's most beautiful hills overlooking the deep dark water of Loch Katrine in Perthshire. The yearly round of lambing, dipping, shearing and the sales is marvellously interwoven into the story of the glen, of Rob Roy in whose house John now lives, of curling when the ice is thick enough, and of sheep dog trials in the summer. Whether up to the hills or along the glen, John knows the haunts of the local wildlife: the wily hill fox, the grunting badger, the herds of red deer, and the shrews, voles and insects which scurry underfoot. He sets his seasonal clock by the passage of birds on the loch, and jealously guards over the golden eagle's eyrie in the hills. Paul Armstrong's sensitive illustrations are the perfect accompaniment to the evocative text.

Mr Barrington is a great pleasure to read. One learns more things about the countryside from this account of one year than from a decade of 'The Archers'.

THE DAILY TELEGRAPH

Powerful and evocative . . . a book which brings vividly to life the landscape, the wildlife, the farm animals and the people who inhabit John's vista. He makes it easy for the reader to fall in love with both his surrounds and his commune with nature.

THE SCOTTISH FIELD

An excellent and informative book . . . not only an account of a shepherd's year but also the diary of a naturalist. Little escapes Barrington's enquiring eye and, besides the life cycle of a sheep, he also gives those of every bird, beast, insect and plant that crosses his path, mixing their histories with descriptions of the geography, local history and folklore of his surroundings.

TLS

The family life at Glengyle is wholesome, appealing and not without a touch of the Good Life. Many will envy Mr Barrington his fastness home as they cruise up Loch Katrine on the tourist steamer.

THE FIELD

The Hydro Boys

Emma Wood

ISBN 1 84282 047 8 PBK £8.99

'The hydro-electric project was a crusade, with a marvellous goal: the prize of affordable power for all from Scottish rainfall'

This book is a journey through time, and across and beneath the Highland landscape . . . it is not just a story of technology and politics but of people. EMMA WOOD

I heard about drowned farms and hamlets, the ruination of the salmon-fishing and how Inverness might be washed away if the dams failed inland. I was told about the huge veins of crystal they found when they were tunnelling deep under the mountains and when I wanted to know who 'they' were: what stories I got in reply! I heard about Poles, Czechs, poverty-stricken Irish, German spies, intrepid locals and the heavy drinking, fighting and gambling which went on in the NoSHEB contractors' camps. EMMA WOOD

Nobody should forget the human sacrifice made by those who built the dams all those years ago. The politicians, engineers and navvies of the era bequeathed to us the major source of renewable energy down to the present day. Their legacy will continue to serve us far into the 21st century. BRIAN WILSON MP, *Energy Minister, announcing a 'new deal for hydro' which now 'provides 50 per cent of the UK's renewable energy output. The largest generator serves more than 4 million customers.'* THE SCOTSMAN

Notes from the North incorporating a Brief History of the Scots and the English

Emma Wood

ISBN 0 946487 46 4 PBK £8.99

Notes on being English Notes on being in Scotland Learning from a shared past

Is it time to recognise that the border between Scotland and England is the dividing line between very different cultures?

As the Scottish nation begins to set its own agenda, will it decide to consign its sense of grievance against England to the dustbin of history?

Will a fresh approach heal these ancient 'sibling rivalries'?

How does a study of Scottish history help to clarify the roots of Scottish-English antagonism?

Does an English 'white settler' have a right to contribute to the debate?

Will the empowering of the citizens of Scotland take us all, Scots and English, towards mutual tolerance and understanding?

Sickened by the English jingoism that surfaced in rampant form during the 1982 Falklands War, Emma Wood started to dream of moving from her home in East Anglia to the Highlands of Scotland. She felt increasingly frustrated and marginalised as Thatcherism got a grip on the southern English psyche. The Scots she met on frequent holidays in the Highlands had no truck with Thatcherism, and she felt at home with grass-roots Scottish anti-authoritarianism. The decision was made. She uprooted and headed for a new life in the north of Scotland.

She was to discover that she had crossed a border in more than the geographical sense.

Loving her new life and friends in first Sutherland and then Ross-shire, she nevertheless had to come to terms with the realisation that in the eyes of some Scots she was an unwelcome 'white settler' who would never belong. She became aware of the perception that some English incomers were insensitive to the needs and aspirations of Highland communities.

Her own approach has been thoughtful and creative. In *Notes from the North* she sets a study of Scots-English conflicts alongside relevant personal experiences of contemporary incomers' lives in the Highlands. She gently and perceptively confronts the issue of racial intolerance, and sets out conflicting perceptions of 'Englishness' and 'Scottishness'; she argues that racial stereotyping is a stultifying cul-de-sac, and that distinctive ethnic and cultural strands within in Scottish society are potentially enriching and strengthening forces. This book is a pragmatic, positive and forward-looking contribution to cultural and politicial debate within Scotland.

Notes from the North is essential reading for anyone who is thinking of moving to Scotland and for Scots who want to move into the 21st century free of unnecessary baggage from the past.

Desire Lines: A Scottish Odyssey

David R. Ross

ISBN 1 84282 033 8 PBK £9.99

A must read for every Scot, everyone living in Scotland and everyone visiting Scotland!

David R Ross not only shows us his Scotland but he teaches us it too. You feel as though you are on the back of his motorcycle listening to the stories of his land as you fly with him up and down the smaller roads, the 'desire lines', of Scotland. Ross takes us off the beaten track and away from the main routes chosen for us by modern road builders.

He starts our journey in England and criss-crosses the border telling the bloody tales of the towns and villages. His recounting of Scottish history, its myths and its legends is unapologetically and unashamedly pro-Scots.

His tour takes us northwards towards Edinburgh through Athelstaneford, the place where the Saltire was born. From there we head to the Forth valley and on into the Highlands and beyond, taking in the stories of the villains and heroes through Scottish history.

Pride and passion for his country, the people, the future of Scotland; and his uncompromising patriotism shines through *Desire Lines*, David R Ross's homage to his beloved country.

Ross' love for his native heath and depth of knowledge is second to none.

THE SCOTSMAN

David Ross is a passionate patriot. He is not afraid of stating his opinion, and he does so with unabashed gusto. The result is an enlightening travel book.

SCOTS MAGAZINE

On the Trail of Bonnie Prince Charlie

David R. Ross

ISBN 0 946487 68 5 PBK £7.99

On the Trail of Bonnie Prince Charlie is the story of the Young Pretender. Born in Italy, grandson of James VII, at a time when the German house of Hanover was on the throne, his father was regarded by many as the righful king. Bonnie Prince Charlie's campaign to retake the throne in his father's name changed the fate of Scotland. The Jacobite movement was responsible for the '45 Uprising, one of the most decisive times in Scottish history. The suffering following the battle of Culloden in 1746 still evokes emotion. Charles' own journey immediately after Culloden is well known: hiding in the heather, escaping to Skye with Flora MacDonald. Little known of is his return to London in 1750 incognito, where he converted to Protestantism (he re-converted to Catholicism before he died and is buried in the Vatican). He was often unwelcome in Europe after the failure of the uprising and came to hate any mention of Scotland and his lost chance.

- 79 places to visit in Scotland and England
- One general map and 4 location maps
- Prestonpans, Clifton, Falkirk and Culloden
- battle plans
- Simplified family tree
- Rarely seen illustrations

Yet again popular historian David R. Ross brings his own style to one of Scotland's most famous figures. Bonnie Prince Charlie is part of the folklore of Scotland. He brings forth feelings of antagonism from some and romanticism from others, but all agree on his legal right to the throne.

Knowing the story behind the place can bring the landscape to life. Take this book with you on your travels and follow the route taken by Charles' forces on their doomed march.

Ross writes with an immediacy, a dynamism, that makes his subjects come alive on the page.

DUNDEE COURIER

Scotlands of the Mind

Angus Calder

ISBN 1 84282 008 7 PBK £9.99

Does Scotland as a 'nation' have any real existence? In Britain, in Europe, in the World? Or are there a multitude of multiform 'Scotlands of the Mind'?

These soul-searching questions are probed in this timely book by prize-winning author and journalist, Angus Calder. Informed and intelligent, this new volume presents the author at his thought-provoking best. The absorbing journey through many possible Scotlands – fictionalised, idealised, and politicised – is sure to fascinate.

This perceptive and often highly personal writing shows the breathtaking scope of Calder's analytical power. Fact or fiction, individual or international, politics or poetry, statistics or statehood, no subject is taboo in a volume that offers an overview of the vicissitudes and changing nature of Scottishness.

Through mythical times to manufactured histories, from Empire and Diaspora, from John Knox to Home Rule and beyond, Calder shatters literary, historical and cultural misconceptions and provides invaluable insights into the Scottish psyche. Offering a fresh understanding of an ever-evolving Scotland, *Scotlands of the Mind* contributes to what Calder himself has called 'the needful getting of a new act together'.

Angus Calder has proved himself one of the most sophisticated thinkers and writers on this gleaming new Scotland . . . any selection of his work [is] full of surprises and pleasures . . . 'Scotlands of the Mind' is magnificently diverse, ranging over subjects like chatter in the pub.

THE SCOTSMAN

The complexities of national identity are eloquently addressed here.

THE LIST

Reportage Scotland: History in the Making

Louise Yeoman

Foreword by Professor David Stevenson

ISBN 0 946487 61 8 PBK £9.99

Events – both major and minor – as seen and recorded by Scots throughout history.

Which king was murdered in a sewer? What was Dr Fian's love magic?

Who was the half-roasted abbot?
Which cardinal was salted and put in a barrel?
Why did Lord Kitchener's niece try to blow up Burns's cottage?

The answers can all be found in this eclectic mix covering nearly 2000 years of Scottish history. Historian Louise Yeoman's rummage through the manuscript, book and newspaper archives of the National Library of Scotland has yielded an astonishing range of material from a letter to the king of the Picts to in Mary Queen of Scots' own account of the murder of David Riccio; from the execution of William Wallace to accounts of anti-poll tax actions and the opening of the new Scottish Parliament. The book takes pieces from the original French, Latin, Gaelic and Scots and makes them accessible to the general reader, often for the first time.

The result is compelling reading for anyone interested in the history that has made Scotland what it is today.

Marvellously illuminating and wonderfully readable.

Angus Calder, SCOTLAND ON SUNDAY

A monumental achievement in drawing together such a rich historical harvest.

Chris Holme, THE HERALD

Luath Press Limited
committed to publishing well written books worth reading

LUATH PRESS takes its name from Robert Burns, whose little collie Luath (Gael., swift or nimble) tripped up Jean Armour at a wedding and gave him the chance to speak to the woman who was to be his wife and the abiding love of his life. Burns called one of The Twa Dogs Luath after Cuchullin's hunting dog in Ossian's Fingal. Luath Press was established in 1981 in the heart of Burns country, and is now based a few steps up the road from Burns' first lodgings on Edinburgh's Royal Mile. Luath offers you distinctive writing with a hint of unexpected pleasures.

Most bookshops in the UK, the US, Canada, Australia, New Zealand and parts of Europe either carry our books in stock or can order them for you. To order direct from us, please send a £sterling cheque, postal order, international money order or your credit card details (number, address of cardholder and expiry date) to us at the address below. Please add post and packing as follows: UK – £1.00 per delivery address; overseas surface mail – £2.50 per delivery address; overseas airmail – £3.50 for the first book to each delivery address, plus £1.00 for each additional book by airmail to the same address. If your order is a gift, we will happily enclose your card or message at no extra charge.

Luath Press Limited
543/2 Castlehill
The Royal Mile
Edinburgh EH1 2ND
Scotland
Telephone: 0131 225 4326 (24 hours)
Fax: 0131 225 4324
email: gavin.macdougall@luath.co.uk
Website: www.luath.co.uk